DIRHAM

'Nothing is Impossible'

SHAHUL VALAPATTANAM

Cover Design: Muhammed Arshad
Cover photo: Sahil Hameed

Contents

Contents

CHAPTER 1

In the sterile whiteness of the hospital room, Nandakumar found himself surrounded by the harsh glow of fluorescent lights, which rendered everything stark and hyper-real. Doctor Ali's voice suddenly pierced the stillness of the room. "Nothing to worry about," he assured, his tone both clinical and comforting. "This back and neck pain's a common ailment here in the Gulf."

Doctor Ali sat back down, drying his hands after washing them carefully at the washbasin. "You sit staring at the computer screen all day. The pain stems from incorrect posture. Sit erect, look straight at the screen, and ensure you stand and stretch at least every half an hour. It's also wise to take a walk around the office before returning to your seat."

Seated across from him, Nandakumar absorbed every word, nodding slightly, the room's silence amplifying each syllable. His relationship with Doctor Ali had evolved over a decade, beginning with a cold treatment when he first moved to Dubai. Their rapport had deepened with each visit, reflected in the doctor's detailed explanations and evident fondness for his long-time patient. As Doctor Ali scribbled on the medical claim form, he looked up abruptly. "Nandan, have you stopped going to the gym? You used to be regular."

Caught off guard, Nandakumar's face flushed with a mix of embarrassment and resignation, "I hardly find the time. Office responsibilities have grown incredibly demanding."

Doctor Ali's laughter filled the room, rich and unabashed. "We're all strapped for time. Look at me, I haven't even found a moment for a proper shave recently." Only then did Nandakumar notice the unkempt beard on the doctor's face, and laughter soon echoed his, a moment of lightness in the clinical environment.

One week had passed since that reassuring conversation. As Nandakumar was leaving, Doctor Ali offered one more piece of advice. "The tablets and ointment I've prescribed will help, but they're not the whole solution. Try incorporating yoga into your routine, along with your other exercises, if you can."

Such recommendations were part of Doctor Ali's repertoire, aimed to impress and perhaps ensure a return visit. Yet, he seemed distant from the daily struggles that Nandakumar faced, the pace of his professional life that left little room for such prescriptions.

Each morning, as he entered the office, a pile of files marked 'urgent' flooded his desk. He had to scrutinize each document thoroughly and forward them to the General Manager with his annotations. The GM, reliant on his assessments, would swiftly decide on these matters, often without further deliberation. The responsibility was immense; a minor oversight on Nandakumar's part could wreak havoc, impacting his career and the General Manager's decisions.

While most of the staff clocked in at eight, performing their tasks with a casual eye on the clock, eager for the day to end at six, Nandakumar's reality was different. He often arrived well before the official start, foregoing lunch breaks and the chatter of colleagues. Instead, he sipped black coffee brewed by the office boy, a meagre substitute for a midday respite. His day stretched long after others had departed, a solitary figure against the backdrop of dimming office lights, racing against time to clear the day's workload. If not, he faced the daunting prospect of an even more overwhelming tomorrow.

Despite the grind, Nandakumar's life, at least on the surface, appeared enviable. His paycheck surpassed that of anyone else in the company, and his home in Emirates Hills, a sprawling villa, spoke of his success. He drove a latest model of Mercedes-Benz, a machine that turned heads on Sheikh Zayed Road, and his bank accounts in Dubai and back home reflected years of his labor.

Vacations took him to corners of the world most could only dream of, a passport heavy with stamps from countries as varied as Switzerland and Samoa. Late-night dinners at the Burj Al Arab and Atlantis had become familiar rituals, occasions filled with impeccable service and menus that read like poetry. From the outside, his life seemed gilded, each detail a hallmark of someone who had "made it."

But success had its costs, and Sushama, his wife, reminded him often. "Nothing excuses neglecting your health," she would say. Her words echoed Doctor Ali's from the week before: "You've got to prioritize your health. There's been a drastic shift in your test results." The doctor had insisted he step on the clinic's weighing scale, and the numbers hadn't lied. "Your weight has gone up significantly. You can't keep ignoring this," Doctor Ali had warned.

In the quiet of his office, Nandakumar glanced at his cell phone. The screen glowed with the time: 8:15 p.m. The file on his desk demanded immediate attention, a document that had to reach the General Manager by morning and then move to the Board Chairman. Leaving it unfinished wasn't an option.

"Sir, would you like more coffee?" The office boy stood at the door, his face eager but careful, as if not wanting to intrude. After finishing his rounds of cleaning with Dettol spray, the boy lingered each evening, wiping desks and workstations until they gleamed. It was an order from the GM to stay until Nandakumar left, a precaution to ensure he had everything he needed.

For the boy, the arrangement had its perks. Every extra hour waiting outside Nandakumar's door translated into generous overtime pay at the end of the month. He didn't mind lingering in the cool, clean air of the office while others had long gone, leaving behind the scent of freshly polished floors and the faint sounds of the central air conditioning. To him, the overtime felt like a quiet victory, one small triumph in the shadows of another man's larger, noisier success.

The cell phone vibrated softly against the desk, its subtle buzz like a persistent whisper. Nandakumar had long since silenced its ringer, a precaution born of the General Manager's disdain for interruptions during meetings. On days when he forgot, the consequences were immediate: a sharp glance, a shift in the GM's tone. To avoid such lapses, he'd started muting the phone first thing each morning, a small ritual that had become as routine as his first cup of black coffee.

The screen lit up, displaying Sushama's name alongside a photo of her smiling, radiant against a backdrop of golden light. This was her third attempt to reach him. He hadn't answered the first two calls, knowing exactly how the conversation would begin. Her voice, soft but impatient, would ask the same question it always did after six: "When will you come?"

This time, he decided not to risk it. Ignoring her again meant enduring a frosty silence later at home, a penance he could no longer afford. He grabbed the phone hastily, clearing his throat as if rehearsing.

"Hi, honey."

That word always worked. Sushama had a weakness for it, a balm that softened even her sharpest rebukes.

"I'm just stepping out," he said, injecting a practiced warmth into his voice. "I'll be there within half an hour."

Her reply came quickly, brisk and resolute. "Alright, get here soon. I didn't make anything for today. Let's go out for dinner." She hung up without waiting for him to respond, her tone leaving no room for negotiation.

He stared at the phone for a moment, its screen now dark. Sushama's temper could flare, but beneath it lay an undeniable tenderness. He couldn't fault her frustration. Each evening, he arrived home late, worn out and silent. Their conversations, if they could be called that, had dwindled into perfunctory exchanges, words uttered more out of habit than connection. By the time he finished his hurried dinner, all he wanted was the oblivion of sleep.

She had every right to be irritated. Sushama spent her days in the silence of the villa, a silence broken only by the sounds of the television or the click of a mouse. There was only so much time one could devote to scrolling the internet or watching reruns of shows that had long lost their charm. The kitchen, which might have provided some distraction, offered little solace; the part-time maid handled most of the chores, leaving Sushama with hours that stretched into an unbroken monotony.

She often said she was bored out of her mind. With no close friends in Dubai, there were no coffee outings, impromptu shopping trips, or lively conversations to punctuate her solitude. Her days blurred together, marked only by the household routines and the distant sound of Nandakumar's car pulling into the driveway late each evening.

Fridays and Saturdays, when his office officially gave him a break, should have been their time together. But Nandakumar had a habit of slipping into the office on one of those days, intent on clearing his desk of tasks that couldn't wait. This, more than anything, was a source of constant tension. Sushama would confront him as he prepared to leave, "Why do you have to go in today? It's supposed to be your day off."

When he stayed home, her requests were modest enough. She wanted to step out at least once or twice a week, a chance to escape the confines of the villa. More often than not, their outings led to one of Dubai's sprawling malls, a destination he had come to associate with a peculiar kind of weariness.

The drive itself felt like an ordeal. Traffic on Dubai's roads was unyielding, the kind of congestion that tested even the most patient drivers. The thought of inching his way through packed streets filled him with dread. Once they reached the mall, another challenge awaited: the hunt for a parking spot. He would circle the multi-level lots, his frustration growing with every loop before finally slotting the car into a space far from the entrance.

Inside, they joined the throngs of people walking through polished corridors. They rarely bought anything, preferring to linger in front of glittering storefronts, watching displays they had no intention of taking home. Occasionally, they caught a movie at the multiplex, a brief reprieve from the crowds. One ritual remained constant: the visit to the food court. Fast food trays laden with burgers, fries, and soft drinks seemed to bring Sushama a momentary satisfaction, her expression lightening as she savored the meal.

For her, these outings were enough to stave off the dullness of her days. For him, they were another demand on a schedule that had little room to accommodate even such small joys. Each visit to the mall felt like a task checked off his growing list of responsibilities, but he could never escape the guilt of knowing how little time he truly gave her.

Nandakumar pushed back his chair and stood, stretching his shoulders to ease the stiffness from hours at his desk. The room felt colder now, the air-conditioning constant against the glass walls. He walked to the window and pulled the blinds aside with one hand. The city stretched before him, a vast, glowing grid, its pulse unchanged no matter the hour.

From the twentieth floor, the view was unmatched. New Dubai unfolded in a single sweeping frame, with glass towers reflecting the glow of streetlights, cranes frozen mid-motion against the skyline, and the distant shimmer of the marina. Below, Sheikh Zayed Road buzzed with movement. Headlights flickered in endless succession, a slow-moving river of light, every vehicle locked in its own quiet urgency. Cities like this came alive at night, their real conversations unfolding in the rush of traffic, the glow of late-night diners, and the murmured exchanges between those who, like him, were leaving work long after they should have.

He reached for his jacket, slinging it over one shoulder, then straightened his tie with a quick, practiced motion. His cell phone and iPad rested on the desk, the last things he grabbed before heading out. Just as he reached the door, the office boy appeared, standing in the threshold as if unsure whether to speak.

"I'm leaving," Nandakumar said, out of habit. The boy knew the routine. Once Nandakumar was gone, he could shut down the office and head home.

But tonight, something was different. "GM has come," the boy said, voice low.

Nandakumar frowned. "GM? He left in the evening. Told me we'd meet tomorrow."

The office boy shifted, hesitating for a moment before repeating, "He just walked in. Asked me to let you know if you were still here."

Nandakumar exhaled sharply, the weight of exhaustion settling deeper into his bones. "Of all times," he muttered, not bothering to lower his voice. "Not a minute's break since morning, and now, just when I'm about to leave…"

He tossed his jacket onto the chair and placed the cell phone and iPad back on the desk. After one last glance out the window at the city, still moving with its mechanical precision, he turned and headed toward the GM's office.

This was strange. The GM never returned at this hour. If it was urgent correspondence, that meant trouble. Last-minute drafting, revisions, and approvals awaited him, and his night was about to go haywire. Sushama would be waiting, expecting him to walk in so they could leave for dinner. She had already said she hadn't cooked. He could see it now: the dinner plans falling apart, disappointment flickering across Sushama's face as the evening unraveled completely.

The GM's door was closed. Nandakumar knocked, then waited. The pause on the other side stretched longer than expected.

Finally, a voice came from within, calm and clear.

"Yes, come in."

CHAPTER 2

The GM sat still, his eyes locked on the laptop screen, though it was obvious he wasn't actually reading anything. His fingers rested above the keyboard, frozen in place. The dim glow of the screen lit up his face, revealing the tension on his features. He didn't look up or react to Nandakumar's arrival, seemingly unaware that someone had entered the room.

Nandakumar hesitated, and this wasn't like him. The GM had always been the kind to acknowledge every arrival, to stand and shake hands, to ask how things were before getting to the point. No matter how many times they met in a day, there was always a polite greeting and a brief moment of formality before business took over.

Now, there was nothing. No movement, no words. His posture was stiff, his focus elsewhere. Something weighed on him.

Nandakumar shifted slightly, waiting. Whatever had brought the GM back at this hour wasn't routine.

Had he made a mistake? Nandakumar couldn't shake the thought, even though it didn't seem likely. He was meticulous, checking every file thoroughly, reviewing every document before leaving his comments, and never walking away from unfinished work, even if it meant staying late after everyone else had gone home. But mistakes had a way of sneaking in, a misplaced number, a missed clause. No matter how careful he was, he wasn't completely immune to error.

Or maybe the GM was annoyed about being here so late. He preferred to leave as early as possible, delegating everything to Nandakumar and knowing it would get done without follow-up. That had always been the arrangement. Nandakumar worked behind the scenes while the GM took credit in front of the management. It was this instinct for self-preservation, this ability to claim the spotlight without doing the heavy lifting, that had propelled him forward.

The Egyptian had started as a salesman, one among many, but he had moved up with a quiet kind of shrewdness. He understood the game, knew how to step into a room and make people listen.

Still, tonight felt different. He was distant and preoccupied. Nandakumar stood there, waiting for him to speak, for some indication of why he had called him in at this hour.

"Kumar, please have a seat," the GM said, his voice measured, almost too calm.

He was the only one who called him that. The name had been shortened out of necessity since Nandakumar was too much of a mouthful for him, but over time, Nandakumar had grown to like it. There was something familiar about it, something easy.

He sank into the chair across from the GM's desk, though "collapsed" might have been a better word to describe it. His body ached from hours spent hunched over his desk, and the biting cold in the room only added to his discomfort. The GM always kept the air conditioning at the lowest possible setting, a fact the staff often whispered about in hushed tones. They joked that he must have thick skin, the kind that could endure sitting in a freezer without so much as blinking.

The GM let out a long exhale, his eyes still fixed on the laptop screen. Then, without warning, he spoke, breaking the silence in the room.

"I hate this."

The words hung in the air, echoing off the walls.

Nandakumar hesitated. He wanted to ask what the GM meant, but something about his tone made him hold back. There was a heaviness in the room, a sense that whatever this was, it wasn't open for discussion. The GM's expression was unreadable, his gaze fixed somewhere beyond the desk, beyond the moment.

"What can I do?" the GM said, almost to himself. Then, in a clipped, resigned tone, "It's part of my job. Whether I like it or not." Nandakumar studied him. The GM never spoke this way. There was always authority in his words, an assurance that whatever decision was being made was the right one. But now, there was something else. A careful distance, an apology woven into the edges of his voice.

"What is the matter, sir?" Nandakumar asked. "What happened?"

The GM slid an envelope across the desk.

"Trust me," he said. "I have nothing to do with this."

Nandakumar reached for the paper, his hands trembling slightly. It felt heavier than he expected, as though it carried the weight of something irreversible. Slowly, he unfolded it, his eyes catching the bold official letterhead at the top.

It only took a moment for the words to sink in. Everything around him seemed to pause—the quiet hum of the laptop, the chill in the air, the faint creak of the chair he was sitting on. His vision dimmed at the edges, his mind struggling to comprehend the reality of what he was reading.

It was a termination letter.

The Chairman himself had signed it. The words at the start were polite but cold. "The management regrets to inform you that…" He couldn't finish the sentence. His eyes welled up, and the text blurred into an unreadable haze.

There was no explanation. No reason given. Just a cold, formal statement informing him that his services were no longer required. The letter offered nothing beyond that— no accusations, no performance issues, nothing he could grasp onto. The only certainty was the notice period. Thirty days to wrap up everything, clear his desk, and hand over his responsibilities to whoever the company decided would take over.

Nandakumar read the letter again, searching for something he might have missed. The words remained the same. His mind refused to accept them.

His voice came out unsteady. "What's this, sir? What have I done to deserve this?"

The GM pushed back his chair and walked over, stopping just beside him. He placed a hand on Nandakumar's shoulder, his grip firm but without reassurance.

"It's not your fault, Kumar," he said. "The board met at Burj Al Arab. This was their decision. Given the situation, they didn't see another way."

Nandakumar felt his breath hitch, his throat dry.

"But why me, sir? Why?"

He wanted to say more, to spill the emotions building inside him, but the words stuck in his chest, locked under the pressure of it all. It was as though the enormity of the moment had rendered him silent.

The GM returned to his chair and sank back, resting his elbows on the desk. His fingers tapped lightly against the surface, a habit Nandakumar had noticed before, usually when he was weighing his words.

"You know what's happening, Kumar. The financial crisis is spreading. It hasn't fully hit the Gulf yet, but it's coming."

Nandakumar sat stiffly in his chair, his posture tense. He had seen the headlines and overheard the whispers in the corridors, but none of it seemed to explain why he was now sitting across the desk, holding a termination letter in his hands. He met the manager's gaze. "I understand that, sir. But what does that have to do with me? I need to understand why I'm the one being let go. What did I do wrong?"

The GM exhaled as he responded, "The company is cutting costs. They've decided to restructure. Senior employees with high salaries are being replaced by new hires on lower wages." He paused, then looked directly at Nandakumar. "Your name was the first on the list because you're the highest-paid."

"So that's it?" Nandakumar's voice was quieter now. "Everything I've given to this company, all the hours, all the work, none of it matters?" He held the GM's gaze. "You've told me yourself how valuable I am. More than once, you said I was the most efficient employee here."

The GM lifted a hand, cutting him off before he could say more. "Don't take it that way. The company is making adjustments before the recession takes full effect. This has nothing to do with your performance." He paused for a moment, studying Nandakumar's face before continuing. "I argued in the board meeting. Told them losing you would be a huge loss, one we wouldn't recover from easily." He shook his head slightly. "The Chairman shut it down, asking how an exception could be made for one employee when a company-wide policy had already been decided."

Nandakumar knew better than to respond. The words sounded rehearsed, the kind of justification a man gives when he has already chosen his side. The GM had a way of staying in the good graces of people. It was a skill, the ability to appear concerned while ensuring he remained untouched.

Nandakumar had no concrete proof that the GM had pushed for this decision, but there was something in his tone, in the way he distanced himself from the responsibility, that made it obvious. Whether he had initiated it or merely let it happen, the outcome remained the same.

The GM folded his hands together as he continued, "Don't worry, Kumar. You have time to look for something else. The company won't cancel your visa immediately."

He said it like it was a favor, as if the extra time was some kind of compensation for years of service.

Nandakumar rose slowly, the rolled termination letter pressed tight in his palm. His legs felt unsteady beneath him, each step requiring more effort.

None of this had been foreshadowed. There were no warning signs, no whispers in the corridors, no changes in management's behavior that might have tipped him off. The layoffs themselves weren't the real shock. He had seen the news, read the reports about Europe, America, China, and Japan. The crisis had reached every corner of the world. He just never thought it would reach him here in Dubai, a city that always seemed untouched by the instability affecting everywhere else.

He stepped out of the GM's office, the air in the corridor feeling colder than before. His cabin was just a few steps away, but the distance felt stretched. When he reached his desk, the cell phone was already vibrating. He didn't need to check the screen to know who it was.

Sushama.

She had called three times earlier, and he had promised to be home in half an hour. It had been well over an hour now. He could picture her in the living room, phone in hand, glancing at the clock, wondering why he hadn't answered.

"Idiot." The word left his mouth before he could stop it. His voice, sharp and bitter, cut through the silence of the empty office. He had been proud of this job, of the salary that put him ahead of other Keralites, of the title that gave him a certain standing. And now, just like that, none of it mattered. The company had discarded him with the same ease that one might delete an old file.

Sure, the pay had been good. But hadn't he earned it? Hadn't he delivered? He had pushed himself past exhaustion, ignored the ache in his back, the stiffness in his neck. He had done everything asked of him, and then more. And still, they had handed him that letter, as if none of it had meant anything.

The cell phone buzzed against the desk again, the vibration breaking through his thoughts. He knew he had to pick it up this time. If he didn't, Sushama would be furious, not just because he was late but because he had ignored her calls.

He took a deep breath and answered.

"What happened? Are you stuck in traffic? Or did you go somewhere else? You do this all the time, tell me to wait and then get caught up in something else."

The words tumbled out of her, sharp and relentless, leaving no space for him to respond. He gripped the phone tighter, pressing his fingers into his temple. The last thing he needed was an argument, not now. He swallowed the anger rising in his throat and forced his voice to stay even.

"I was about to leave when the GM showed up," he said. "Something serious came up. I'll be late."

Sushama's voice hit him like a slap. "Why don't you just stay there with your GM and spend the night?"

Nandakumar clenched his jaw. The words burned, not because they were unexpected, but because they were timed too well. She had a way of pushing when he was already at the edge.

"Great idea," he said, his voice colder than he intended. "Call the restaurant and order something. We're not going out tonight."

A sharp breath came from the other end, then silence. The line went dead.

He dropped the phone onto the desk and leaned back, his eyes fixed on the ceiling. His pulse still thudded in his ears. Going home now would be a mistake.

Sushama would be waiting. Pacing the floor, arms crossed, ready to unleash her anger the second he walked in. And once she saw his face, once she caught the way his shoulders sagged, the way his eyes looked hollow, she would know. She wouldn't need to ask. She would sense it.

Then the questions would come, followed by the panic and the anger, directed squarely at him, not the company. Why had he let this happen? Why hadn't he seen it coming or tried to fight back? And worst of all, the moment she'd pick up the phone to call her parents in Abu Dhabi. By morning, they'd be involved. Her father would demand answers. Her mother would offer advice in that pitying tone she couldn't quite hide. He wasn't ready for any of it.

Nandakumar didn't let himself think. He picked up his cell phone and dialed.

The call barely had time to ring before Johnny answered, his voice loud, laced with amusement.

"What's this? A call from you at this hour? That's a first. What happened—your wife ran off with someone?"

Johnny had been saying it for years. That one day, if Nandakumar kept working like this, Sushama would get fed up and leave. "You spend your life in that office, man. One day, you'll come home and find she's packed her bags." It was always a joke. Until tonight, Nandakumar wasn't sure why it stung.

"I need to talk," he said. "There is something serious."

The shift in tone wasn't lost on Johnny. They had known each other too long. There were few things they couldn't read in each other's voices.

"Nandan," Johnny said, the humor gone, replaced by something heavier. "What happened?"

Nandakumar swallowed, his fingers tightening around the phone.

"I got it too," he said. "The sack."

Johnny didn't follow at first. "What?"

"Listen, you son of a gun," Nandakumar said, his voice rough. "I'm out. They kicked me out. I don't have a job anymore."

Johnny was silent for a beat, then let out a short, disbelieving laugh. "Come on, man. That's not funny. Why would they fire someone like you?"

Something in Nandakumar cracked. The weight of it, the hours spent pretending to hold it together, the way everything had unraveled in the span of a single evening. It all hit at once. His breath caught in his throat, and before he could stop himself, the sobs came. Guttural, raw. He pressed his hand over his mouth, but it was no use.

"Efficiency," he choked out. "Bullshit. None of it means anything."

He squeezed his eyes shut, but the words of the termination letter still burned against the back of his mind. The board had met. A decision had been made. And at the very top of the list, before anyone else, before they had even hesitated, was his name.

CHAPTER 3

Without much thought, Nandakumar suggested 'Lal Mirchi' for the meeting with Johnny. It was their place, the default choice for Thursday nights when the weekend began and the city loosened its tie. By evening, the restaurant would be packed, every table claimed well in advance. The waiters would move fast through groups of men with loosened collars and women in silk kurtas, while the rich aroma of tandoori spices and charred meat lingered around them. Glasses were endlessly refilled, the liquor flowing without pause, as conversations ebbed and flowed in sync with the soulful melodies of Ghazals performed by visiting maestros.

But tonight was different. The city outside still held its weekday pace, the streets full of cars rushing home instead of people settling in for the long, unhurried hours of a Thursday night. Johnny was in his car when Nandakumar called.

Johnny took a breath before answering. "Not Mirchi," he said, firm but even. "Meet me at Dubai mall." It was a habit, one he never broke. Drinks were for weekends. Weekdays had their own order: work, dinner, home. No detours. Even on Thursdays, when he drank, he never lost control. Two, maybe three drinks, always spaced out, always with food. He liked the ritual of it, the small discipline that kept everything in check.

Nandakumar wasn't willing to change his mind. "I need a drink, Johnny. My head won't stop pounding."

Johnny sighed. "Sushama's waiting. Go home, take a shower, and lie down. You'll feel better."

"I already told her I'd be late. She won't wait for me. She'll eat and go to bed." Nandakumar sounded certain, like the matter had been settled long before this conversation.

Johnny had nothing left to say. He checked the road ahead, flipped on his indicator, and made a slow U-turn toward Lal Mirchi. The traffic was thinning out, the sky darker now. The headlights of passing cars reflected in his side mirror, streaks of white and red stretching down the road.

When he reached the restaurant, the neon sign glowed dimly above the entrance. It wasn't as crowded as it would have been on a weekend, but there were enough people inside, voices overlapping and the clinking of glasses breaking through the steady flow of conversation.

Johnny moved between the tables, his eyes scanning for Nandakumar. They always chose a quiet spot in the farthest corner, a little secluded from the rest of the diners, giving them enough distance from the noise without feeling completely shut out. If Nandakumar was here, that's where he'd be.

He was right. Nandakumar sat slumped over the table, his head bowed as if the weight of it was too much to bear. An empty glass stood on the table beside his scattered belongings: car keys, mobile phone, and wallet.

Johnny pulled out a chair and sat down. The smell of liquor hit him immediately, sharp and heavy. It curled into his nose, turning his stomach in a way it never had before. He wanted to walk out, leave before the weight of the night settled on him too.

"Nandan, what's all this?" Johnny's voice was more of a plea than a question. "Why did you have to drink so much? You know how this works. People lose jobs in the Gulf all the time. You'll find another one."

Nandakumar shook his head slowly, his fingers gripping the edge of the table. His voice was rough when he finally spoke. "No. This is different." His words were heavy, as if he was forcing them out. "I never saw it coming. I never even thought…" His voice faltered for a second before he continued. "How do I tell Sushama? And what happens when her parents find out?"

Johnny reached across the table, "Just stay calm. We'll figure out how to reassure Sushama. You shouldn't feel guilty; this wasn't your fault."

Nandakumar was silent for a moment. Then, without a word, he reached into his wallet and pulled out a stack of credit cards. He laid them down one by one, their gold and silver surfaces catching the dim light of the bar, sparkling subtly.

"Look at this, Johnny. Every one of these is overdue. I've been paying the minimum for months, and the interest has piled up. On top of that, I have my bank loan. The EMI goes out every month like clockwork."

Johnny stared at the cards, his mind struggling to catch up. This was the first he was hearing of it. For as long as he could remember, Nandakumar had spoken about his salary with a quiet kind of pride. He never flaunted it outright, but it was always there, in the way he spoke about his car, his house, the vacations. It had been impossible not to feel a twinge of envy. They had studied together, graduated together, and arrived in Dubai within months of each other. But while Johnny had spent years working his way up, Nandakumar had landed a job that paid more from the start.

Johnny couldn't shake the discomfort gnawing at him. Nandakumar's life sparkled with the trappings of success: a villa in Emirates Hills, a Mercedes Benz in the driveway, a beautiful wife by his side. In contrast, Johnny's own life seemed modest. He was still single, living in a shared apartment, commuting in a Toyota Corolla. But they were best friends. Envy had no place between them. Yet, sitting across from Nandakumar now, Johnny felt a pang of guilt. His chest tightened. "Oh God, what am I doing?" he muttered under his breath. "Am I secretly pleased to see him like this?"

Pushing aside these unsettling thoughts, he focused on the man in front of him. "Nandan, I had no idea about all this. I thought you were just piling up savings. Where's all your money going?"

Nandakumar picked up his glass again, the ice cubes clinking against the sides as he swirled it, draining the last few drops. "I've never told anyone this. I bought a plot in Kochi, right next to the upcoming Smart City. It seemed like a smart investment. Expensive, sure, but I figured it'd pay off." He set the glass down harder than he meant to. "I used everything I had, plus some hefty loans. I still need to pay off half before I can even think about registering for it. And now, with the job gone…" His voice trailed off, his eyes not meeting Johnny's.

Johnny's emotions swirled. He was hurt that Nandakumar had kept such a significant decision, a plot of land, a dream, from him, his best friend. A part of him whispered that perhaps this was divine retribution for keeping secrets. God wouldn't forgive such actions, he thought bitterly.

Yet, he masked his turmoil with a calm, empathetic tone. "Don't worry, Nandan. We'll figure something out. Maybe we can find a buyer for the land. Property values in Kochi are climbing every day."

"No!" Nandakumar's voice cracked through the air, his fist clenching. "I won't let that plot go. It's a dream. I can't bear the thought of it belonging to someone else."

Johnny bit back his immediate reaction, the wave of frustration at Nandakumar's stubbornness. He smoothed his expression and spoke in even tones, though inside, his feelings churned. "That's your call, Nandan. But we should call it a night now. You still have to go to the office tomorrow. Remember, any missteps during your notice period could cost you your gratuity and benefits."

The cell phone buzzed, rattling against the table. It rang long enough to demand attention, then stopped abruptly, leaving behind an uneasy silence.

Johnny questioned, "Why didn't you pick it up?"

Nandakumar let out a short, humorless laugh, saying, "It's her. Sushama. She must've called a hundred times by now. I told her to go to bed, but that dumb head wouldn't listen."

Johnny frowned. "Why are you blaming her? She's your wife. She's worried because you're out late, and she has no idea what's going on."

Nandakumar looked away, his jaw tense. "Worried? For what? She's part of the reason this is happening." He rubbed his temples as if trying to push away the thought. "She's unlucky, Johnny. Some people bring fortune, and some don't."

Johnny let out a sharp laugh, shaking his head. "Oh, so you lost your job because Sushama isn't lucky enough? Nothing to do with the economy crashing, the company cutting costs, just bad luck from your wife?" He scoffed. "That's ridiculous."

He pushed back his chair and stood, reaching across the table. His grip was firm as he clasped Nandakumar's wrist. "Nandan, you've become unbearable tonight. I don't want to see you like this. This isn't you."

The words seemed to settle something in Nandakumar. He pushed back his chair and got up, slow but silent. For a moment, Johnny thought he was steady enough, that maybe he hadn't had as much to drink as he'd assumed. But as soon as Nandakumar took a step, Johnny saw it: his balance was off, his movements just a second too slow, too careful. He had misjudged. Nandakumar must have already downed more than a few drinks before he got there.

Johnny reached out instinctively, slipping an arm around his friend's back to steady him, but Nandakumar pulled away.

"I won't fall, Johnny," he muttered, keeping his head high, his voice firm. "If I fall, that's when you help me."

Johnny let his hand drop but stayed close. He watched as Nandakumar reached for his wallet, his fingers moving deliberately as he pulled out cash and placed it on the bill tray. He counted it twice, nodding slightly, before following Johnny toward the exit. Outside, Johnny handed his valet ticket to the man at the counter and waited. A breeze cut through the night, carrying the smell of damp pavement.

The valet returned a moment later, but instead of bringing Nandakumar's car, he simply shook his head. "Sir, he didn't use the valet." Johnny turned to Nandakumar, who stood a few feet away, already heading toward the parking lot. "Of course, you didn't," Johnny muttered under his breath as he followed.

The parking lot was quiet except for the echo of footsteps and the occasional sound of a car engine humming to life in the distance. Nandakumar moved with a sluggish determination, his keys already in his hand. Johnny quickened his pace, catching up to him. "You shouldn't drive like this. You know what happens if *Shurta* catches you for drunk driving. Just leave the car here. I'll give you a ride."

Nandakumar waved off Johnny's concern with a dismissive hand. "No, I'll manage. Don't you know I started driving at an early age? I'm experienced enough to handle the car in any condition."

Johnny watched him stagger slightly as he approached his car, disbelief and worry knotting his stomach. As Johnny climbed into his own car, he couldn't help but think, "How conceited!" It was a thought that often crossed his mind when Nandakumar boasted. "Nandan will never change. He's wrapped up in self-praise, convinced he's perfect, looking down on everyone else as if they're lesser beings."

Johnny started his car, pulled away from Mirchi, and merged onto the main road. As he glanced at his reflection in the rearview mirror, he noticed a slight furrow in his brow. A flicker of guilt ran through him. What am I doing?

Nandakumar is his friend. No one was perfect. He had flaws, but so did everyone else. And no matter how frustrating he could be, he had always been there for Johnny when it mattered. There were times when he had helped without being asked, times when he had lent money and never brought it up again. Johnny exhaled slowly, shaking the thoughts away.

His hand instinctively made the sign of the cross and a quiet prayer slipped from his lips.

Lord, this could be me tomorrow.

The thought sent a shiver through him. Dubai was shifting. Companies were cutting costs, trimming their workforce without hesitation. If Nandakumar, efficient, well-paid, respected, could lose his job overnight, what chance did he have?

Johnny's family back home depended on him. Every month, his salary made its way to them, keeping their lives steady. His father's medicines, his mother's hospital visits, his sister, who was already old enough to be married but had no savings of her own, his younger brother still in school; everything ran on what he earned. If the money stopped, their lives would unravel.

A heavy weight settled on his chest. He tightened his grip on the steering wheel, his knuckles turning pale.

O God…

The words formed silently before he let them out in a whisper. "Protect me. Let me keep my job."

The roads stretched before him, glowing under streetlights that flickered as if they too were uncertain of what tomorrow would bring.

Chapter 4

Nandakumar meant every word about his driving. His hands stayed firm on the wheel, his eyes refused to flutter closed. On Sheikh Zayed Road, his car felt more like a bullet than a machine on tires. The city lights, scattered across concrete and glass, gave the night a faint pulse. The traffic around him pushed forward, horns and headlights tracing lines along the highway. Dubai pulsed at all hours.

He kept the speedometer climbing. The posted limit was 120 kilometers per hour, and he knew radar cameras gave grace until 140. Past that point, the flash would come, and the fines would grow. Six hundred dirhams for a small breach—an amount that matched a laborer's monthly pay. Nandakumar was aware of how that money got earned under a sun that scorched shoulders and burned through hope. He guessed the radar had captured him more than once tonight, maybe twice or three times. The fines would total in the thousands, and he had no salary to cushion him now.

A bitter taste crept up his throat from the drinks. He remembered the cornflakes at breakfast, the cookies at midday, black coffee he had used for fuel when work kept him chained to his desk. He reached over to the passenger seat for his water bottle, only to find it drained. His annoyance flashed white-hot for a second. He flung the plastic toward the back seat. The car swerved, and a horn blared from behind. He pressed his foot down, stayed in the fast lane, and did not look back.

The flyover from Sheikh Zayed Road toward Emirates Hills crept along at a snail's pace. Cars inched forward in both lanes, their headlights reflecting off concrete barriers. Nandakumar shifted lanes whenever he spotted a gap, weaving past slow-moving sedans and trucks. He had learned how to handle a car when he was a teenager, back when he slipped his father's keys off the living room counter and drove around the neighborhood late at night. In college, he had grown bolder and took friends' luxury cars for joyrides.

He remembered enrolling in driving school soon after reaching Dubai. He knew it could drag on for years to earn a license, but he cleared every stage in three tries. The official who administered the test seemed ready to fail him, yet found nothing to criticize. He eventually started with a modest car and moved on to the Mercedes that now carried him through the city. He believed nobody outdrove him.

When he finally parked, he staggered into the villa, switching on a single light. The place felt silent. He imagined Sushama walking through each room in the evening, turning switches off one by one, growing more irritated with each unanswered call. The dining table held unopened food containers. He guessed she had lost her appetite. A pang of guilt kicked in. He slid the packets into the fridge without making noise, then headed to the bedroom.

He felt his breath catch as soon as he saw her. She lay on the bed turned slightly to the side, hair scattered over the pillows, nightgown gathered around her waist. He had never stood like this, watching her sleep, while a dull throb moved through his temples and a foul taste lingered in his mouth. He recalled something she used to tease him about: "I hate to see you drunk. You seem more alive between the sheets when you have a little liquor in you, though." He let the memory pass. He thought of waking her, then changed his mind. The day had drained them both. He fumbled with his shirt buttons, feeling the room spin a bit, and told himself tomorrow might look different once the sun rose.

Nandakumar settled beside her, the scent of her night cream drifting up into his face. She always smoothed it over her skin before turning off the lights, and he could feel that soft, slippery texture under his fingers. He slipped an arm around her, pulling her close. She murmured something, though she didn't move away. Her breath warmed his neck through the thin fabric of her nightgown. He let his hand roam across her shoulder and along her back, then rested it on her hip. He felt her shift in response. That gave him courage to guide her onto her back and press his body over hers.

Blood thrummed in his veins, an echo to the urgent pulse of his heart. She seemed to share the same intoxication, their bodies entwined tightly. His lips traveled fervently across her neck, arms, and face, fueled by her soft moans that spiraled the intensity higher.

The room faded around them, and he felt as if they were alone in the midst of a tempestuous sea. Their movements became more vigorous, like waves rising high before crashing against the shore with force, only to retreat and gather strength again. He kissed her with a passion that felt like swimming against a strong current, pushing forward with all his energy.

For a moment, he believed he could reach safety, the shore was within sight. But suddenly, as if caught by an undertow, his limbs weakened. A gasp escaped him, his breaths short and desperate. The waves of reality closed in, overwhelming him, pulling him back from the brink of escape. Exhaustion seeped into every muscle, anchoring him in place, making each movement feel like a battle.

Hot, sharp thoughts cut through the haze of passion. The GM's voice rang out, a harsh dismissal, "You don't need to work anymore." Johnny's mocking laughter haunted him, sharp and stinging, "You're sacked. Nandan, see what happened to your hefty salary now?" Calls from Kochi pierced through, each one a reminder of his looming obligations, "What about the deed registration? Where is the remaining money?"

Each echo in his mind was a wave crashing over him, dragging him further from the shore he so desperately sought, leaving him adrift in a sea of turmoil and loss. His muscles refused to cooperate, and his energy vanished like water swirling down a drain. She groaned, shoved him off, then scrambled to the edge of the bed. "Such a waste of time!" she snapped. "Why try when you couldn't make it?"

He stayed where he was, facedown, heart racing from shock and shame. He had never faltered like this before. He heard her in the bathroom, muffled words bouncing off the tiles. Anger rose in his chest. "What are you blabbering in there? Come here and say that to my face!"

She opened the door a crack. "If this happens again, I'm leaving. That's it!"

His mind spun as she slammed the door. He lay there, staring at the dim ceiling, breath ragged. Shame clung to him like a damp sheet, and he told himself morning might dull the sting.

Chapter 5

Chandran Nair sat in the conference room of Al Saeed Construction Company on Naif Road, arms folded on the table's edge. He looked at the three senior staff members gathered around him, then said, "Why are you all silent?"

Chief Accountant Sathyamurthy, Engineer Sadashivam, and Estimator Salahuddin stared at one another but said nothing. They had weathered many company crises by Chandran Nair's side, and he counted on their judgment. Today, they offered no words.

He glanced through the tall glass window framed by drawn curtains. Noon light fell across Naif Bazar, yet the street below was strangely quiet. He saw fewer shoppers than usual, a thin trickle that made the emptiness feel stark. The shops looked deserted, shutters half-open without the steady hum of trade.

Naif Bazar once burst with color and noise. Africans and Iranians filled the sidewalks, buying goods in bulk for re-export. There was heavy traffic every day at this hour, but now he counted a single pickup here and there. The dry air seemed to carry a warning. Chandran Nair sensed the global recession was no longer a distant threat. Dubai's commerce felt the strain, and the city's edges were beginning to fray.

He remembered his recent conversation with the bank manager, who had said, "It's a dire situation, Mr. Nair. The Central Bank is imposing stringent measures to prevent collapses we've seen abroad." Then came the final blow. "Your overdraft facility is cancelled. Everything withdrawn must be repaid soon, as these overdrafts had no collateral."

Chandran Nair tried to ignore the weight on his chest. He had always trusted that funds would materialize once client bills got settled. Al Saeed Construction Company employed more than a thousand workers, and its local sponsor had lent a name but never any capital. Chandran Nair bore the full responsibility. He tapped his fingers on the table, scanning the silent faces of his senior staff, wondering how he would keep the company afloat.

Chandran Nair looked at the documents in front of him and thought about the official requirement: the Arab sponsor held fifty-one percent, and the foreign partner held forty-nine. In truth, the sponsor collected a fixed fee for yearly license renewals and stayed away from profits or losses. Everything else fell on Chandran Nair's shoulders.

He repeated, "Don't just sit there staring like that. Share whatever ideas you have."

Sathyamurthy cleared his throat and said, "Let's not focus on the discontinued overdraft facility right now. Our immediate crisis is how to repay what we've already overdrawn. We don't have that kind of money in hand."

Sadashivam added, "All five projects are near completion. We need a large quantity of materials for the final phase. We can't expect further payment from the owners until we hand over the completed buildings."

Murthy nodded. "Which means we have to buy those finishing materials ourselves. No trading company will offer credit in these circumstances."

Chandran Nair turned to Salahuddin. "I need you to calculate how much material is required and how much cash we'll need."

"We have to wrap up these projects on time," said Sadashivam. "We accepted them with thin profit margins. Any delay leads to extra expenses."

Chandran Nair thought about the new projects and spoke under his breath, "If only we could start those soon. The advance payments would help us stay afloat." He knew his company had quoted the lowest price for those tenders, and he was waiting for the work order.

Murthy reminded him, "month end is almost here. We have to pay wages. We'll need a big sum for that too."

"Let's explore if we can obtain funds through alternative means," Chandran Nair said. Though he spoke with confidence, no idea came to mind. He felt as though the progress he had built over the years was little more than a structure floating on air. He had pushed forward on sheer determination, with a bit of luck to ease the way. Now, headlines everywhere talked about the recession hammering businesses in America and Europe. Banks had lent carelessly, debtors failed to repay, and the entire system crashed under its own weight.

He recalled the old joke: when America catches a cold, all other countries sneez. That was happening now. The crisis had rolled out from the States to Europe and then on to the rest of the world. At last, it reached the Gulf, a region people once considered untouchable by financial trouble.

After he dismissed the meeting, Chandran Nair returned to his office and slid into his chair. He pulled a worn diary from his drawer. While Murthy and his team tracked most records on computers, Chandran Nair had always kept his personal notes in this diary. He leafed through the pages. The company's bank balances were low, and every anticipated payment had dried up. Meanwhile, they owed money to suppliers and ready mix providers, and payday for the workforce was right around the corner.

He thought back to when he first arrived in the Gulf. He was barely more than a boy, crossing dangerous waters on an illegal launch that threw him overboard. He had believed he was close to shore, though he wasn't. He knew how to swim, which saved his life that day. He reached land after a fierce struggle. Now, as he looked at the numbers in his diary, he felt a pang of déjà vu. He braced himself to wade into yet another tide that threatened to pull him under.

Chandran Nair's life after reaching shore was an ongoing battle. Like countless newcomers to the Gulf, he endured hardships and moments of despair. Back then, this region lacked modern conveniences, and he took whatever work he could find. He started by carrying bricks at a construction site. Over time, he took on modest sub-contracts for shuttering, steel, and block work with a Pakistani friend from that same site.

His projects expanded slowly, and he started a small contracting firm. Fifteen years passed before it grew into the established company he oversaw now. He had always prided himself on paying his workers at the start of every month. He wondered how he would maintain that tradition in the coming weeks. Delaying payments to suppliers seemed possible, but not covering wages for laborers who toiled under the punishing sun felt unthinkable. There was also the risk of intervention by the Labour Department if any salary payments fell behind.

He remembered how some construction companies once ran three or four months late, leaving employees with unpaid balances. That practice was no longer an option under the newer WPS system. A single missed month triggered an automatic alert, and the Department blacklisted the company. After that, there was no way to secure new visas or renew existing ones.

Chandran Nair thought about possible ways to raise money, though banks had shut their doors to him. He reflected on how he had managed some loans by giving considerable tips to the manager. The odds of that working now seemed slim, and he was left with a heavy feeling that another tide of trouble was closing in.

The bank manager was an Iraqi who had come here with his family when Saddam's war made it impossible for them to stay in their homeland. He demanded bribes for every favor but gave out funds without security. That path was now blocked.

Chandran Nair thought about reaching out to those he had helped in the past. He had provided assistance in different ways over the years, though he wasn't sure if anyone would offer him the same consideration now. Still, he decided to try.

His phone rang. The receptionist said, "Sir, there's a call from Union Consultancy."

He felt a moment of unease. "Connect it, please," he told her, although he wondered why they were calling. He remembered the commission he had given their manager to secure two projects.

He sensed the consultancy manager's reluctance on the other end. "Is there any problem, Sir?" Chandran Nair asked.

"We had intended to award both projects to your company," came the reply. "You can see how conditions are these days, though. Both projects are on hold. The owners can't get bank loans like before. It used to be possible to borrow eighty or ninety percent of the contract value, but the new rules tie everything to land value—"

Chandran Nair stopped listening. He muttered, "Oh God," placing both hands on his head. Those two projects had been his lifeline. He was counting on the advance payments they would bring, but everything had slipped out of reach. "What an awful day," he said. "Nothing but bad news?"

Chapter 6

It was still dark outside, with time left before the Fajr prayer. A jolt made Usmanikka open his eyes, as though someone had roused him. He stayed still, waiting for his vision to adjust. Through the faint light, he noticed Hamza sprawled on a mattress in the corner, snoring loudly, face turned into the pillow.

Hamza was the only other person sharing that cramped space. He had shown up after losing his job, with no set responsibilities. He handled errands for Usmanikka and drove him whenever needed. There was no fixed salary—he lived there without paying rent, and he ate without spending on food, in exchange for cooking duties. He was an excellent cook, known for tasty meals.

Hamza was a cheerful soul with a knack for causing trouble daily, earning him a routine scolding. He seemed to grin through the complaints, though, and over the short time they had been together, a warmth had grown between him and the older man.

When Usmanikka tried to sit up, his body refused, and he sank back on the bed. His muscles no longer responded the way they had for seventy-three years. Mornings brought a piercing pain that traveled from his feet to his head. Sometimes Hamza would ask, "Ikka, why stay in this foreign land when you could go home to your children and grandchildren?"

"Get lost, you stupid guy!" he would reply, though his tone was filled with a fond exasperation.

It was true that Hamza's comment sounded naive because this place never felt foreign to Usmanikka. He had arrived at eighteen, crossing the sea in a launch. Fellow travelers had gaped at the sight of a teenager. Some said, "Go back. This is dangerous. Who knows if you'll even reach shore? Even if you do, what chance do you have there?"

He stayed firm. He had a streak of defiance, especially toward his father, who was known in their region for his part in the Mappila Revolt. The man loved to talk about a scar left by an English bullet, though Usmanikka was unsure if the story was real.

He felt no pride in a father who only spun tales while the family starved. The children often went hungry. The man never accepted help from anyone, not even government aid. He declared he hadn't risked his life for money but for the rights of poor farmers.

Hearing this used to rile Usmanikka. He would answer back, forgetting any respect owed to a parent. His blood, shaped by Eranad's fierce history, ran hot. Determined to forge his own path, he sought out the Muslim Khalasis in Kozhikode for work, guided by someone from his village. Through that contact, he met the crew who ran launches to Dubai.

Several passengers lost their lives during the journey from hunger and disease, while others were thrown overboard and drowned. Still, young Usman emerged from that peril, his determination forged in early hardship. He never accepted defeat, and his trust in Allah always carried him through.

Usmanikka managed to rise slowly and slipped his feet into his flip-flops. The nearby bathroom saved him precious minutes in his busy routine. Every moment counted.

He owned a modest cafeteria in Meena Bazar, tucked away behind a row of textile shops in Bur Dubai, where business thrived despite its quiet location. Another bustling spot stood in Deira Gold Souk. In addition, he ran a laundry in Hamriya, leased to a resourceful Bihari, and two small grocery stores, one in Satwa and the other in Aweer. He had also leased Arab villas, partitioned them, and rented them out to several tenants. Each opportunity was a blessing, and he gave thanks every day.

The day never seemed long enough to manage all his ventures. With countless routine tasks and unexpected challenges demanding immediate decisions, he stayed involved in every detail of management. His hands-on approach was essential to keeping the businesses profitable, leaving little time for rest.

"But why am I still working so hard? For whom?" The question echoed in Usmanikka's mind, the same way it did every morning as he slouched in front of the washbasin, brushing his teeth. His children were long settled, with families of their own—some with grandchildren already growing up. He had done his duty, ensuring that those with academic potential received a good education and that those drawn to business had the means to set up their own ventures. His daughters were married into respectable families, their futures secured.

At some point in that journey, his wife had left this world. It had been a mild chest pain, nothing alarming at first. She spent three days in a nursing home while he remained tangled in work in Dubai. By the time he managed to reach home in Kerala, it was too late. She had passed, and there was nothing left to do but mourn.

She had been the thread that tied him to their children. After her, that thread frayed, and the distance between them widened. They rarely called. When they did, it was out of courtesy. If they needed something, they would speak with warmth, but once their needs were met, silence would follow again.

As he stepped out of the bathroom, the Azaan for Fajr prayer rang through the early morning air. Four mosques surrounded the villa, all built by citizens who had donated land to the Waqf Board. Their calls for prayer overlapped, merging into one thunderous chorus.

Despite the deafening summons, Hamza still had to be nudged awake. Usmanikka tapped his foot against the younger man's hip, shaking him lightly. "Hamza, they've called for prayer… Get up quickly."

Hamza stirred but didn't wake, which only annoyed Usmanikka further. When frustration crept in, he never called him by name. Instead, he used *hamk*, the word for a fool. He gave him a sharper nudge with his toe.

"You *hamk*, any plans to wake up yet? Or should I pour water over your head right here?"

That did it. Hamza shot up, blinking in confusion, his head jerking from side to side as if trying to place himself. The sight of his bewildered face melted Usmanikka's irritation. A smile twitched at his lips before he gave in and laughed.

Still chuckling, he reached for his *qantoora*, slipping it over his shoulders, then set his skullcap firmly on his head. His hand instinctively reached into the *qantoora's* pocket for his thasbiya, the smooth beads familiar between his fingers.

For years, this had been his attire—the simple, flowing robe, the cap, the prayer beads in hand. Anyone looking at him would assume he was an Arab. There was nothing in his dress or mannerisms to suggest he was from Malabar, and his Arabic was fluent enough to pass without question.

He caught Hamza in a sidelong glance, watching as the younger man stumbled toward the bathroom in a hurry. *Hamk!* he thought with amused affection. *He never wakes up on time. Now he'll half-brush his teeth, splash some water over himself, and rush to the mosque just as the prayer begins.*

No matter how many times he advised him, Hamza refused to sleep early. He would stay up watching television late into the night, only to get scolded when he finally switched it off.

Outside, the night still clung to the sky. The streetlamp cast a pale glow into the front yard, its light pooling over the tiled ground. Usmanikka stepped onto the path and walked toward the gate, fingers slipping one bead after another as he murmured, *Subhanallahi Wa Bihamdihi Subhanallahil Azeem...* His voice was low, steady, threading through the quiet air like a whisper to the divine.

CHAPTER 7

The alarm clock rang at precisely 4:30 a.m., just as it did every weekday. Friday was the only exception. Gopalakrishnan relied on that sharp metallic ring to pull him out of sleep—any later, and he would be late for work.

Most people had long replaced alarm clocks with cell phones, but he preferred the old-fashioned kind. He had tried using his phone before, but more than once, when the alarm blared, he had groggily picked it up and muttered "Hello," thinking it was a call. Padmavati had caught him doing it several times, doubling over with laughter. She would shake her head, teasing, "This is what happens when you cross fifty."

That was when he decided to buy a proper alarm clock. During a shopping trip to Global Village at the Dubai Shopping Festival, he picked out a classic one—Roman numerals, thin black hands, and two small domes at the top.

He could hear Padmavati moving around in the kitchen, the clang of utensils against the stove. She always woke up before him, slipping into her routine before the house had fully stirred. Breakfast had to be made, tiffins packed for their two school-going boys, and lunch prepared for Gopalakrishnan to take to the office.

In between, she had the impossible task of dragging their sons out of bed.

The boys were in tenth and eighth grade, but when it came to waking up, they were worse than kindergarteners. Getting them to rise and get ready for school was an ordeal, one that started with soft nudges and ended in stern warnings.

A loud crash of utensils hitting the floor jolted Gopalakrishnan awake. He usually liked curling up under the covers for a few extra minutes, letting the morning ease in. But the sudden noise shattered that small luxury. He sighed, irritated. *O God! When will Padmavati change? She storms around the kitchen like a thundercloud, and this is how she lets it out? By throwing things around!*

He knew her morning routine wasn't endless. She only had to manage the rush for a couple of hours, getting breakfast ready, packing lunch, and nudging the boys into their uniforms. Once everyone left—him for work and the children for school—she had the house to herself. She could nap, watch TV, or chat on the phone for as long as she liked.

His own schedule felt far more punishing. Office hours started at eight, but his day began at 4:30 a.m. It took him nearly two hours to reach work at Al Quoz in Dubai from their flat in Sharjah. It wasn't because of distance but because of the relentless morning traffic.

Dubai rents were steep, beyond the reach of most middle-income workers. Sharjah offered cheaper housing, but that came at the cost of long, grueling commutes. Every morning, thousands made the same journey. Roads from Sharjah to Dubai were choked with cars. In the evenings, the lanes reversed and were packed with people returning home.

On top of it all, he couldn't head straight to work. First, he had to drop the kids at their school in Garhoud. In the evening, he would stop by again to pick them up. It was an extra hassle, but it meant saving on the school bus fee. That, at least, was something.

By the time he reached the office, crawling through the sluggish traffic, he felt drained in both body and mind. It was even worse on his way back home. All he wanted was to eat dinner and go to bed early. That was necessary because he had to rise before dawn the next day.

He had no option but to accept these difficulties if he hoped to cover household expenses with his modest salary. He paid the flat rent, school fees for the children, costs for private tuition, water and electricity bills, car fuel, food for the family, and still managed to send money to relatives back home.

Gopalakrishnan took a shower, got dressed for the office, and sat down at the dining table. Padmavati's raised voice spilled out from the children's room. She was scolding them, as usual.

"Look at that boy next door. He wakes up by himself and studies, and his mother doesn't have to drag him out of bed. He gets ready for school on his own. He stands first in every exam and listens to his mother. He isn't like you two good-for-nothings!"

Her younger son fired back, "You forgot something. His parents take him on a foreign trip every year. Have you taken us anywhere? He has an expensive phone, and we don't even have cheaper ones."

The older son added, "He also gets pocket money. We just get lectures: 'Look at him, learn from him.'"

Padmavati must have felt hurt by their words. She stepped out of the room with the look of someone who had lost a battle. She spotted Gopalakrishnan at the dining table and realized he had been listening all along. That turned her anger on him.

"Oh, so you were here, hearing everything? You don't have one word to say to these brats? Have you swallowed your tongue?"

Gopalakrishnan spoke softly, worried the children might overhear him. "Let it go. They are just kids. They will change as they grow older."

Padmavati's voice turned shrill. "Kids, you say! You do not see how selfish they already are. When they grow up, they will pack you and me off to some old age home. I am certain of it."

She returned to the kitchen as the boys came out with their school bags. Gopalakrishnan leaned in and spoke to them in a low voice, making sure Padmavati could not hear. "Your Amma is saying all this because she cares about you. You should listen to her quietly instead of arguing."

His older son, Gireeshan, said, "This is too much, Achha."

Pradeepan, the younger one, added, "You deserve a medal, Achha, for putting up with her nagging all these years."

Gopalakrishnan raised his hand playfully as if to strike them. Father and sons shared a close bond, and Padmavati often complained, "The three of you gang up together and leave me out. If only I had two daughters, they would have understood me better."

When Padmavati emerged from the kitchen, she wore a calm face with no sign of the earlier quarrel. She helped her children with their breakfast and kept an eye on her husband so he would not overeat. She reminded him, "You are getting older. You should watch what you eat."

He agreed with her as he drove the children to Dubai. He was aging, and the company rules said he must retire at sixty. His visa could be extended until sixty-five, but the company was not interested. They saw no benefit in retaining an older employee when energy often waned by that age.

Gopalakrishnan once held a permanent job in Kerala, though it did not pay much. He resigned and spent money on a visa to come to Dubai. He had a BA degree, and his acquaintance Razak, who ran a cafeteria in the city, arranged a cook's visa for him. Razak also promised to help him get a "release" if he found another job, allowing him to stay in Dubai on a new visa.

After arriving, he searched everywhere for decent opportunities. He used to think a BA degree was a good qualification, and he also had typing skills. It did not take long to realize these were not enough for a well-paying job.

In the end, he found something, even though the salary was small. He needed a release to switch from his cook's visa to the company's sponsorship. Razak said the Arab sponsor demanded money for signing those papers. Gopalakrishnan could not tell whether Razak was honest or trying to extract more from him.

He paid the amount, which increased his debts further. He had borrowed money for rent and food while searching for a job in Dubai. He had also taken loans before arriving, to cover his visa and flight ticket. Even after finding employment, it took him nearly two years to clear everything he owed.

The Emirates Road from Sharjah to Dubai was packed, and cars moved at a snail's pace. The bigger challenge was dealing with drivers who changed lanes abruptly in an attempt to overtake. A small slip in attention could lead to a crash. If that happened, Gopalakrishnan would have to pull over and wait for the police to show up and issue a ticket. He would be late for the office, and his children would lose class hours.

"I have a test in first period," said his older son, Gireeshan. "If I am late, I will end up waiting outside the classroom."

"Don't worry," Gopalakrishnan said, hoping to calm him. "We should reach on time. Though I do wonder why we have stopped all of a sudden."

"Maybe there is an accident ahead," his younger son suggested.

Gopalakrishnan felt a throbbing ache in his neck. The pain had started a few days ago, adding to the back trouble he had dealt with for a long time. Even a short drive seemed to worsen it. He rubbed his neck with one hand and steered with the other. In that moment, a pickup sped past and cut in front of him. He tried to brake, but his foot hit the accelerator by mistake. The car lunged forward and slammed into the pickup with a loud crash.

Fortunately, nobody was hurt, though the front of his car was crushed. He stepped out, and the Pakistani pickup driver let out a stream of angry words. Gopalakrishnan was certain the driver was at fault for swerving without warning, yet the police would probably fine him for failing to keep enough distance. He asked himself how anyone could maintain distance when traffic moved so slowly and cars were bunched together.

Ignoring the driver's shouting, he took out his phone and dialed 999 to call the Traffic Police. He had to wait for them to arrive and issue a ticket. His children complained that they would miss class, and he told them he would lose half a day's salary too. His workplace used a time clock system. Even a five-minute delay meant half a day's pay gone.

Chapter 8

He felt embarrassed by the quiet satisfaction he felt over Nandakumar's job loss. He had tried to comfort his friend, yet deep down he thought that God had punished Nandakumar for showing off.

He and Nandakumar had been friends since childhood and went through college together, studying the same course in the same batch. Johnny moved to Dubai first, and Nandakumar came soon after. Johnny believed that in the Gulf, luck was more important than qualifications or experience, though hard work could shape how far a person went.

Johnny had stronger academic records and more practical experience back home than Nandakumar, but Nandakumar ended up with the higher-paying role that came with generous perks. Anyone might envy such a position, though Johnny wondered if it was right to feel jealous of a friend's success.

He lifted the office memo from the desk again and scanned its contents. The words seemed to yell at him, and he felt he deserved it. He saw it as a kind of divine punishment for feeling glad over his friend's loss instead of showing real sympathy.

The memo contained a proposal, describing the company as a family that did not want any staff member to leave during the financial crisis. It explained that this was why they were making the suggestion.

"What fine words," Johnny thought, though it felt like a dagger hidden behind a polite smile. The memo said employees would face a small pay cut starting next month because of the crisis, with an assurance that the old salary would be restored when things improved. It asked everyone to sign the attached document to confirm acceptance.

He checked his new salary, which was thirty-five percent less than before. The company called this a minor reduction, and he shook his head at the choice of words.

Apart from reducing salaries, the company decided to provide flight tickets for vacations only once every two years instead of annually. Several other allowances, such as fuel, parking fees, and cell phone recharge, were also cut back.

Johnny understood the company hoped that employees like him would quit on their own. The organization did not see them as irreplaceable, and the warm language about family seemed more like a formality. If people decided to leave, the company could easily hire new workers who would accept an even lower salary. Many job seekers roamed Dubai with their CVs, ready for any opportunity.

The memo gave employees twenty-four hours to decide whether to accept these new terms or to resign and receive their final dues. Johnny could not afford to resign and return home, especially in a recession. Securing another job would be difficult, and he felt that going back empty-handed was worse than any other fate. His family depended on the money he sent each month.

They faced struggles that reminded him of dire scenes in a movie. His salary was their only lifeline. If he lost his job, they would suffer greatly, perhaps even face hunger and poverty. He feared a desperate situation might drive them to heartbreaking decisions including suicide.

He thought of calling Nandakumar to share the news of his own crisis, wondering if Nandakumar would secretly feel satisfied, the way Johnny had felt before. Then he reminded himself that Nandakumar was not that kind of person.

Johnny believed Nandakumar was a good man, although he bragged at times. He was sensitive, partly because his father and older brother had indulged him in childhood, after he lost his mother at a young age. He was also the youngest in a respected family. His father, now retired, had been a government servant, and his brother worked in the government too.

Johnny tried calling Nandakumar, but there was no response. He guessed Nandakumar was tied up with work, wrapping up his tasks before his final day. The shock of losing his job had robbed him of any real cheer.

Johnny flagged down the office boy, signed the acceptance letter, and asked him to pass it along to HR. He knew he needed to adjust his budget and cut costs next month. He was unsure how to manage it, though, since he was already struggling with his current pay.

He saw the recession's effect everywhere. What began abroad was now hitting the Gulf hard. Crude oil prices were down by several dollars, damaging an economy that depended greatly on oil revenue. Dubai itself did not rely heavily on oil, but it did on tourism, real estate, and re-export. All of these had slowed.

"Did you also receive the love letter?" asked Prasannan, the Head of Human Resources. He was over sixty but kept his position through heavy praise of the higher-ups.

Nothing involving staff escaped his notice, since HR handled those matters. Yet he acted ignorant about the memo, referring to it as a "love letter."

That irritated Johnny. "You must already know. Why ask?"

Prasannan placed a hand on Johnny's shoulder. "No. These orders come straight from above. The Arabic-speaking employees spin their own wheels, and the rest of—Indians, Pakistanis, all are left struggling."

"What about you, Sir?" Johnny asked. "Are you affected too?"

Prasannan seemed caught off guard by the question. He had only approached Johnny to clear his conscience, though there was no real need for it.

Before Prasannan could say a word, Johnny went on, "You know we are all here, in this desert, because we can't make enough back home. Some want to earn more than they did before. At least show a little sensitivity when people face setbacks."

Prasannan threw up his hands. "Goodness, I deserved that. It's impossible to console anyone these days," he said, striding off toward his office.

"Idiot," Johnny muttered under his breath once Prasannan was gone.

He thought about how, in earlier times, he might have tossed his resignation in Prasannan's face. His background in marketing would have made it easy to find another position, possibly a better one.

Now, everything was different. Companies were letting workers go left and right, and some had already shut down. He was not confident of finding another job if he left.

Johnny stood up from his desk, reached for his car keys and laptop, and decided to leave early. There was still an hour left before the official end of the day, but he felt he had earned a moment of relief. It was, in some twisted way, a day to celebrate: the day he got the so-called "love letter."

As he descended to the basement in the office elevator, he thought about visiting Lal Mirchi. He told himself it was the best spot to mark the occasion, though he admitted it was strange to celebrate a pay cut when people usually celebrated a raise.

Johnny thought about calling Nandakumar. It felt right to invite him because he had been by Nandakumar's side when Nandakumar "celebrated" losing his job. Besides, Johnny never went to Lal Mirchi alone. Nandakumar always accompanied him, and Nandakumar usually covered the bill, which was helpful for Johnny, who often struggled with money.

After several rings, Nandakumar answered, "Hello, Johnny."

Johnny felt an immediate sense of relief at hearing his friend's voice. Nandakumar was the one person he could confide in without hesitation.

He said, "Nandan, where are you? Want to meet for a drink at Mirchi? I have some news to share."

Nandakumar let out a hearty laugh and said, "You ass, I am already at Mirchi. I have had a couple of pegs."

Johnny was surprised. "So you have made Mirchi your second home, I see?"

Nandakumar laughed again. "Maybe I will someday, but for now, I have only just arrived."

"Is anyone else with you?" Johnny asked.

Nandakumar's laughter echoed through the phone. "Only me and my sorrow."

Johnny joined in. "Then let me bring my sorrow too. We can share them together."

Chapter 9

He hesitated to meet her eyes. The cheerful face he once knew had faded into a sullen expression. She spoke little and gave curt replies to his questions, and she avoided him whenever she could. Sometimes he caught a hint of scorn on her lips, and he sensed her anger had not cooled.

He tried to calm himself. He believed he had done nothing to hurt her. Whatever happened was not his fault, and nothing like it had ever occurred before. He wished Sushama understood. The first time, when he lost his job, he felt such despair that his mind was crowded with thoughts he could not shake. His body failed him because the worry was overwhelming.

Although her displeasure this time was not as severe as before, it still caused him pain. That pain turned into a quiet resentment when he saw how she seemed unwilling to meet him halfway.

Two nights earlier, he was resolved. He went to bed early, and she was already lying down, though she was still awake. He began touching her gently, and at first she did not respond. Then he kissed her lips and neck, and she began to stir. He had not been drinking and had used her favorite lotion, hoping to please her.

He felt a rush in his veins, and her warmth flowed back toward him. Their bodies pressed closer, yet his excitement slipped away too quickly. He found himself panting and struggling to catch his breath. A chill replaced the heat, as though his strength had fled. He felt as if all the air had been let out of him.

"What's wrong with you?" Sushama snapped, sitting up.

His disappointment flared into anger. "There's nothing wrong with me," he shouted. "You are the one holding back. Why are you so distant?"

She let out a short laugh. "Admit it if you can't do it. Don't blame me."

He let his temper spill. "You bloody… shut your mouth!"

He quickly got dressed and rushed out, not waiting for her reply. Without bothering to turn on the living room light, he collapsed onto the sofa, breathing heavily and covered in sweat. He was too exhausted to move, and even grabbing a glass of water felt like too much effort.

He felt defeated. "Oh God," he whispered, "what's happening to me? Losing a job in the Gulf is common. Why am I so consumed by it that it affects me in bed?"

He made up his mind. He would talk to Sushama the next morning, explain that he only needed a little time, and reassure her that it was the strain on his mind, nothing more. He also wanted to tell her that blaming him would solve nothing and would only make it worse.

But by the next day, she was already avoiding him, which made it impossible for him to follow through with his plan. Three days had passed since then.

He was busy at the office, especially with handing over his responsibilities. The person who was supposed to replace him was a junior employee who did not understand any of his instructions and looked lost. Nandakumar knew it was not the new person's fault. His job involved complex duties that were not easy to grasp, especially for someone at a junior level.

The GM had been out of sight ever since handing him the termination letter, probably out of guilt. Nandakumar had worked hard for him, yet the GM was powerless to help now. In fact, the GM had been taking credit for everything Nandakumar achieved.

People in the office were shocked when they learned he was being let go. They knew if it could happen to someone at his level, it could happen to anyone. Management liked this effect. They could say, "Look, we did not spare our top employee. We cannot do anything."

Nandakumar was aware that more than a few coworkers felt a secret satisfaction at his downfall. They had always envied his high pay and perks. He heard them whispering that his dismissal had nothing to do with the crisis, and that it must be because he had been involved in something shady.

He got dressed for work, even though he now hated setting foot there. He had no choice but to finish the notice period.

Breakfast was ready on the table, but Sushama was nowhere in sight. She used to stand by him before he left in the morning, but these days she hid in the kitchen, pretending to be busy.

Before leaving, he went to the kitchen door to say goodbye.

She was washing dishes at the sink and spoke without turning around. "Achhan will be coming by later. It would be good if you could come home for lunch."

Nandakumar worried that she might have told her father everything, which could explain his sudden visit. She often shared every detail of their life with her parents in Abu Dhabi, and those long calls had raised their phone bills.

He asked, "Is there any special reason for his visit? Does he not have work today?"

She said, "I do not know. He must have his reasons."

"All right," Nandakumar replied as he walked off.

From behind, Sushama called out, "If you do not want him to come, I can call and tell him not to."

That remark irritated him, but he held back his anger. It was too early for an argument. He realized that Sushama, once so simple and easily swayed by him, had changed. He understood that his failure with her in bed must have hurt her pride.

He reminded himself that it was not his fault. He had not intended for what happened, and he felt sad about it. He wished she could see that he had been troubled. He was willing to talk things out, but her aloofness hurt him.

When he came home for lunch, his heart pounded. Sushama's father had arrived much earlier, and her mood had brightened at the sight of him. She busied herself laying out dishes and managed to cook her father's favorite ones in the short time she had.

Nandakumar greeted him politely and said, "You could have brought Amma along."

He answered, "I just felt like seeing my daughter. Last night, when she called, I sensed something off in her voice. I worried, so I decided to come without telling her mother."

Sushama said, "Achhan would not listen when I told him everything was fine. Nandetta, will you help me convince him I am perfectly okay?"

Nandakumar felt relieved that Sushama had not disclosed anything about their recent problems to her father. Still, he worried she might reveal something if her father asked too many questions. He decided he needed to calm his father-in-law's concerns.

He said, "Achha, you worry too much because you love her deeply."

His father-in-law laughed. "You may be right. She is my only daughter. Even her mother is not as important to me as she is."

Sushama smiled, looking both pleased and shy. "Achha, you spoil me too much."

When her father left after lunch, Nandakumar turned to her. "You should not have bothered your poor father."

She pulled a playful face. "Why not? He is my father, after all."

"So, does he mean nothing to me?" he asked. "I have always cared for him like my own father."

Sushama suddenly stepped closer, her eyes blazing. For a moment, Nandakumar worried she was about to argue again.

She said in a trembling voice, "Tell me, then, what do I mean to you?"

He gently drew her toward him. "My dear, why ask that?"

She began to cry. "If I matter so much, why did you hide your troubles from me? Why did I have to hear it from someone else?"

He frowned. "What are you talking about? What troubles?"

"That you lost your job. Why did you keep it from me?"

His relief was immediate. At least she was not angry about their issues in bed. But he wondered how she found out he was unemployed. He had planned to tell her when the time felt right.

"How did you find out?" he asked. "I only kept it to myself because I didn't want to worry you."

She gave him a pointed look. "Johnny let it slip when he called, looking for you. Did you really think I wouldn't find out eventually?"

"That idiot," Nandakumar muttered under his breath. Johnny must have avoided telling Nanadakumar out of fear he would be upset that the secret was revealed.

Still, Nandakumar realized Johnny had done him a favor. He had carried the burden of delivering the bad news, sparing Nandakumar from having to break it himself.

Nandakumar hugged Sushama tightly and said "Please forgive me," he whispered.

She buried her face in his chest, relieved to have the truth out in the open. Nandakumar held her closer, feeling that at least one weight had now lifted.

Chapter 10

Sathyamurthy said, "Obama tried a ten-billion-dollar bailout, but it failed. The recession crossed America's borders, and now it has spread to many countries across the world."

Chandran Nair drove along Sheikh Zayed Road, listening to him closely. He kept a watch on the rearview mirror and the side mirrors. The road in front and behind him was nearly empty, and the lanes to the left and right were also clear. There was a time when cars would flash their headlights, then swerve or overtake at high speed.

Back then, everyone seemed busy. Nobody had the patience to wait for anyone else. Now it was the opposite. The hustle was gone. Nearly empty roads, quiet shopping malls, deserted beaches, parks, and movie theaters were everywhere.

Sathyamurthy was in the middle of speaking when Chandran Nair cut him off. "Like Obama, who is going to bail us out, Murthy?"

Murthy paused, as he usually did. He was a cautious thinker and would not speak before running his thoughts through a mental sieve. That trait often saved him from blunders.

Chandran Nair went on, "It looks like we are in trouble. According to the bank manager, we must repay every debt, and there will be no more overdrafts unless we can provide sufficient security."

This was due to directives from the Central Bank to keep banks from folding. The UAE government had also decided to assist banks with insufficient equity by giving them enough funds.

Chandran Nair opened the glove box with one hand and steered with the other, taking out a small notebook that he handed to Sathyamurthy. He asked him to look at the last page. As Murthy checked the figures, Chandran Nair said, "These entries are in my own handwriting. The small balance you see there is all we have."

"This is impressive, Sir," Sathyamurthy said. "The figures match exactly with the cash balance on my computer."

"I've been doing it this way for years," Chandran Nair replied. "In the beginning, I jotted down amounts of only a hundred or two hundred dirhams. It took quite a journey to reach where we are now."

In those early days, the balance column in his diary showed small sums. His first contract amounted to ten thousand Dirhams, which was a significant figure at the time. That job involved shuttering work for a building linked to his own employer. He managed it with help from two Pakistani carpenters, working right alongside them. His confidence carried him through, and he made a profit of five thousand Dirhams.

Over time, he started taking on contracts for blockwork, steel fittings, and tiling, which brought larger profits. Eventually, he secured the entire construction of a small villa, laying the foundation for Al Saeed Company.

He felt that fortune was on his side and believed in God's blessing. The company expanded from small residential jobs to multi-storey buildings, warehouses, and upscale villas. Work required heavy equipment, cranes, and trucks, employing more than a thousand laborers. Profits soared into the millions.

Chandran Nair was satisfied with how far his firm had come. He trusted that his years of hard work had finally paid off. He planned to retire once his son finished his civil engineering degree, stepping back to offer only minimal guidance.

His dreams now felt as though they were falling apart. The economic crisis had battered his company, and he feared he might need to shut it down.

Once he had parked, Chandran Nair climbed from the basement to the office alongside Sathyamurthy. "You mentioned Obama and America," he said. "What is our plan for getting through this?"

Sathyamurthy replied, "That's what I was going to tell you. Since our new projects are on hold, we don't need the entire workforce. We could cancel visas for half of them. That would bring down salary costs significantly."

Chandran Nair felt uneasy. "Is it their fault, Murthy? If we let them go so abruptly, how will they survive?"

"Many companies are already doing layoffs. Our PRO told me the visa cancellation section at the labor ministry is packed. People are flying home in large numbers."

Chandran Nair sighed. "We still need cash to pay them their end-of-service benefits and cover their tickets. We can't just send them away with nothing."

Sathyamurthy frowned. "Perhaps we can reduce those benefits, saying the recession is partly to blame."

Chandran Nair's voice hardened. "I can't do that, Murthy. They deserve their rightful payment. I was once a laborer like them."

They both fell silent as they neared the office. Rumors were already circulating that the business might fold and everyone would lose their jobs.

Inside Chandran Nair's office, Sathyamurthy shut the door firmly. "There is one way to find funds," he began, "but I'm not sure you'd agree to it."

"Tell me, Murthy," Chandran Nair said. "I trust you completely. You have never been just an accountant."

"I know of a private source that offers loans," Sathyamurthy replied. "It's a Marwari lender in the Gold Souk. You can borrow any amount, even in the millions, as long as you surrender your passport for security. But their interest rate is three times higher than a bank's."

"I have thought about that too," Chandran Nair admitted. "But if we take the loan, how do we manage the interest payments each month, not to mention the principal?"

"There is a strategy. We can borrow more than we actually need. The extra money can be used to cover the monthly interest. By the time we deplete that sum, the market should recover, and we can handle the remaining loan."

"All right, we can explore that," Chandran Nair said.

After Sathyamurthy left, Chandran Nair picked up the phone and dialed a number. The phone rang for a while with no response, and he was about to hang up when his daughter answered.

"Why did you take so long to pick up? Where is your mother?" he asked.

"She's probably in the bathroom," she said in a casual tone.

"And what about your brother?"

"No idea. He went out this morning, claiming it was for college."

Chandran Nair understood the hint. He had received notices that his son was not attending classes regularly. He worried about where the boy spent his time each day and wondered how he would ever graduate. He had planned to send him to Bangalore for higher studies, but the boy refused to leave the Dubai, where he had grown up. His mother supported that choice, which made the situation more complicated.

She had argued that foreign universities had campuses in Dubai's Academic City, so their son could study there without leaving the country. She believed it would keep him under their watch.

Ironically, now Chandran Nair had no idea if his son was actually in class. He was buried in business troubles and lacked the time to follow up, and his wife's indifferent attitude made matters worse.

She spent hours at the malls, searching for luxury items. Though she had grown up in poverty, she now wanted only expensive clothes, perfumes, and handbags from Paris. She often took their tenth-grade daughter along, and Chandran Nair worried this would harm his daughter's studies and lead her to copy her mother's habits.

He felt troubled by the realization that his family did not seem to appreciate his sacrifices or recognize how hard he worked to support them. He had spent his earnings freely, but he understood that would soon end.

Just then, Abdu, the office boy, came in with his regular tray of tea. Abdu was the son of the loyal worker, Assainarikka, who had stood by Chandran Nair through years of effort. When his father retired and went back home for good, Chandran Nair hired Abdu in the company. He lacked the qualifications for a higher post, so Chandran Nair offered him the job of an office boy. Despite that, Abdu had his father's honest nature, which Chandran Nair respected.

Abdu acted like a human surveillance camera, reporting every new office development to Chandran Nair. While Chandran Nair sipped his tea, he asked, "Any news, Abdu?"

Abdu answered, "Everyone is on edge, Sir. They are worried about whose head will be rolled next."

Chandran Nair said, "Tell them not to worry. It's just a head. Let it roll."

Abdu roared with laughter, forgetting for a moment that he was in the presence of his boss. Then only Chandran Nair realized he had delivered a decent joke. He laughed along, then stopped to note how fortunate he was to still find humor in such difficult times.

Chapter 11

When Abdu reached the labor camp in Al Quoz, none of his roommates had returned yet. They typically arrived on a company bus later in the evening. At the site, workers often scrambled to board the bus, pushing and shoving in the hope of getting a seat. Exhausted from a day under the harsh sun, no one wanted to stand while traveling. Arguments broke out routinely, yet no one seemed willing to line up calmly.

The chaos made the bus leave later than planned, and it traveled in the slow lane, so it reached the camp late. As a member of the office staff, Abdu rode in a smaller van. That van dropped off other employees at their homes before heading to the camp, since the driver also lived there. Abdu arrived earlier than the bus crowd, which let him use the toilet without a queue. When the bus finally showed up, the toilets always filled up fast.

In the mornings, it was the same. Many workers skipped the bathroom altogether because there was not enough time and space, so they rushed there as soon as they got back in the evening. Abdu changed clothes and went to relieve himself now, remembering how his morning attempt had been cut short by people banging on the door and shouting, "Jaldi karo bhai, jaldi!" He felt it was ridiculous to hurry something like that and had given up then and there.

Life in the camp was not easy. Fighting for basic necessities drained the workers mentally. Government regulations stated that companies had to provide certain facilities, but few followed those rules. Most camps offered cramped rooms with plywood walls and asbestos roofs. At least ten people shared each space, sleeping on double or triple bunk beds, much like berths on a sleeper train. Limited floor space forced many to spend their free time on their beds.

A camp might house five hundred or even a thousand laborers, yet there were often only ten or fifteen toilets. Some workers were fortunate enough to have one of the few air-conditioned rooms. Others spent their nights under asbestos roofs, and the heat radiating from them made restful sleep almost impossible.

The Municipality and the labor ministry had set many regulations for employers. These covered room sizes, occupancy limits, the number of toilets, and the requirement for larger kitchens, dining halls, recreation areas, and sports facilities for workers.

Most companies treated these rules as more of a formality. No one followed them in full. There were occasional inspections, but the fines they imposed cost less than bringing every camp up to standard.

At times, it felt like the laborers were herded like cattle. Authorities had outlawed cramming people into pickup trucks, so the companies used non AC buses instead, which left many laborers short on air and space.

Abdu had showered and was changing when his roommates got back. Most of them were Malayalis, along with two Tamilians and a man from Andhra Pradesh. The Tamilians were sociable, while the man from Andhra tended to keep to himself because he only knew Telugu.

However, the Malayalis were sharp and quick to find humor in any situation. One of them remarked, "Look who's here early, it's the Arbab." Another joked, "He's got his own transport, lucky guy. Not like us common folks."

"Get lost, you dogs," Abdu said silently. Ever since he arrived, he had discovered it was easier to shout back at them in his head, instead of getting into an argument. It gave him a chance to release anger without causing trouble.

He glanced at the cooking schedule on the wall, posted by the room leader, Shekharettan. Each person took turns making dinner for everyone, day by day. Abdu was relieved to see that it was not his night to cook.

Outside, the toilets were surrounded by a clamor of voices. Some people had chosen to squat by the tap near the compound wall to shower, too impatient to wait for a bathroom. Everyone wanted to rinse off, eat, and rest as soon as possible. A day spent under the scorching sun left them caked in dust and drained of energy.

Abdu stepped out into the yard and looked at his phone. He saw five missed calls from his father. His father always called multiple times if Abdu did not answer right away, even though Abdu had tried explaining that a single call was enough. He could only call back once he was off duty.

He dialed his father's number. His father picked up at once. "Abdu, I keep hearing disturbing reports on the

TV and reading about them in the papers. People are returning, companies are shutting down."

Abdu replied calmly, "Yes, there are some problems, but there's no need to panic. The media often plays it up."

"And what about our Chandran Sir? Is he doing okay?"

"Uppachi, there's no issue with our company. Everything is fine."

His father let out a sigh of relief. "So many families depend on that place for their livelihood. If things go wrong, they will have nothing to eat."

After ending the call, Abdu felt uneasy about sugarcoating the truth for his father. Earlier that day, he had overheard Chandran Nair and Salahuddin discussing the company's growing financial troubles. New projects were getting canceled, and many employees seemed likely to lose their jobs.

Abdu had always worked in close contact with Chandran Nair, so he could tell that his boss had changed. Chandran Nair now arrived at the office later than before, even though he used to be at his desk by eight. When he did show up, he left soon afterward.

On the days he stayed, he dodged phone calls by asking the receptionist to handle them, telling callers he was unavailable. He owed money to several people, some of whom had started visiting the office to confront him. Tensions ran high among the staff, who worried whether they would get paid on time or if they might lose their jobs.

Abdu had his own concerns. His sister, Nabeesu, was getting married soon. The engagement had already taken place, and he had told the groom's family that he would come home for the wedding in two months. That date was drawing closer.

He had hoped to ask his boss for a loan to cover wedding expenses, and he also expected his leave salary and airfare for the trip. Now he was unsure if any of that would happen.

He trusted Chandran Nair's goodwill. Chandran Nair held a deep affection for Abdu's father, always recalling the help Abdu's father gave him in tough times, and Abdu believed that warmth extended to him too.

From the kitchen, Abdu caught the sound of raised voices—a familiar, chaotic dispute among the laborers. Their hard lives, stripped of even the most basic comforts, often led to these outbursts. Many had little left for a proper meal after sending money home, and hunger added fuel to their anger.

The arguments always took on a communal flavor. When an Indian clashed with a Pakistani, each side rallied behind their own, without concern for who was right. In fights between Indians, Malayalis would defend a Malayali, Sardars a fellow Sardar, and Tamilians would back a Tamilian. These divisions were so deeply rooted that Abdu thought they would carry on even after death. He decided to ignore the commotion, knowing that sooner or later the police would arrive to break up the disturbance.

Alcohol played a constant role. Illicit liquor from Umm al Quwain found its way into the camp regularly, smuggled by agents who made a living on the side. A little drink was enough to set off a normally calm worker, turning him belligerent at the slightest provocation.

Just a week earlier, a minor spat between a Sardar and a Pakistani had escalated into tragedy. In a burst of rage, the Sardar had grabbed a kitchen knife and plunged it into the other man's chest, killing him instantly. By the time the police arrived, the Sardar had vanished, though several others were detained.

Later that night, as Abdu climbed into his bed and closed his eyes, he found himself questioning his decision. "Why did I come to the Gulf?" he wondered, the thought heavy with regret. His father had never pressured him to leave; it was his own hunger for quick wealth that had driven him across the sea. Now, each night, in the silence after the day's turmoil, he cursed his own greed and lamented the missed opportunities back home.

Chapter 12

The imam rose from the mihrab, his white robe catching the soft glow of the dim light as he turned to face the congregation. Behind him, the worshippers emerged from the stillness of prayer, rising in gentle, synchronized waves, guided by the quiet rhythm of devotion. The imam, a man from Bangladesh, had led them through every step—the measured recitation, the precise bends of the body, the moments of absolute stillness. The men who followed his lead were from different corners of the world—India, Pakistan, Yemen, Sudan. They gathered here five times a day, a small reflection of something larger, their voices merging in the same verses, their foreheads pressed to the same ground. For a brief time, the weight of their names, their passports, their separate fates dissolved.

Usmanikka stayed seated on his prayer rug, watching as they began to leave. Some moved quickly, their minds already shifting back to responsibilities waiting beyond the mosque walls. Others lingered, greeting familiar faces, exchanging murmured words before stepping out. The scent of sandalwood and attar drifted through the air, mixing with the faint musk of prayer rugs.

He let them pass, his gaze steady but distant. He often remained like this, taking a few extra minutes before stepping back into the world. His fingers moved over the worn beads of his tasbih, his lips forming silent prayers. There were things he spoke of to no one—not to Hamza, not to the men he dealt with in business, not even to his children when they called from faraway homes. These thoughts belonged to the quiet space between him and Allah.

The businesses that had once been his pride were slipping. His hands, which had built a life from nothing, felt the slow unraveling of it now. The laundry in Hamriya, leased to a Bihari man with a sharp mind and an easy smile, had stopped turning a profit. Three months of unpaid rent had passed, and though he could have demanded what was owed, he never did. The man was struggling. Everyone was. There was no point in pressing against something already on the verge of collapse.

The cafeterias, once alive with the restless hum of trade, had fallen quiet. Meena Bazar had changed. The families that used to crowd its narrow lanes, running their hands over bright silks and gold-threaded sarees, had begun spending less. The cash that once moved freely now sat tight in people's pockets. At the Gold Souk, where the weight of a single necklace had once meant nothing to the wealthy, even the jewellers had grown cautious. Fewer customers came. Fewer sales happened.

A strange kind of silence had settled over the city— not the silence of peace, but the silence of waiting. A pause before something heavier arrived.

The exodus had drained the life from his grocery stores. Shelves that once needed constant restocking now stood undisturbed for days. The regulars—men who had stopped by after work for a few essentials, women who had picked up provisions with their children trailing behind—were gone. The lower-income families, the ones who had kept places like his running, had packed their lives into suitcases and left for good. Some had whispered their goodbyes, others had vanished overnight, their absence marked only by unpaid bills and shuttered apartments.

Even the villas he had partitioned and leased—once a reliable source of income—were emptying out. The rooms where children had once played, where the smell of home-cooked meals had lingered in the air, were silent now. As the school holidays neared, more families would leave, each departure another cut into whatever security he had left. He had seen people come and go before. But this time, it was different.

He closed his eyes and let his forehead rest lightly against his clasped hands. The words of his prayer came slow, deliberate, drawn from a place deeper than fear. Ya Rabb, give me the strength to endure. Show me the way forward.

Dubai had always been a city of cycles—boom and bust, rise and fall. He had lived through each wave, adapting, rebuilding, pushing forward. He remembered the dark days of the Iran-Iraq war, when oil prices had wavered, and businesses had stumbled under uncertainty. He had seen the Gulf War when America had gone after Saddam, watched construction sites grind to a halt, salaries slashed, businesses shut overnight. Those years had been difficult. But nothing, not war, not embargoes, not even the times when Dubai had seemed to hold its breath, had felt as ominous as this.

This was something else.

This was the whole world unraveling at once.

Banks, the very institutions that had built empires, had crumbled. Governments that once spoke with certainty now hesitated, their reserves drying up. Jobs, homes, futures—wiped out as if they had never existed. Dubai had always been a land of reinvention, but if this storm lasted, what would remain to be rebuilt?

Ya Rabb, what will happen to all the lives that depend on this land?

A hand on his shoulder. Light, hesitant.

"Usmanikka, shall we make a move?"

Hamza's voice, soft but insistent, pulled him back. The mosque, once filled with murmured prayers and shifting bodies, was nearly empty now. Only the faint scent of musk and the distant hum of traffic beyond the walls remained.

Usmanikka straightened, exhaling slowly. His hands moved over his knees as if grounding himself before rising to his feet.

"Hamza," he said, his voice quieter than before, "do you know how Dubai came to be what it is? How it climbed to such heights from nothing?"

Hamza looked at him, puzzled, his brow furrowing as if he wasn't sure whether this was a question or a lesson.

"And now," Usmanikka continued, his voice tightening, "how can we even begin to imagine its fall?"

For a moment, Hamza didn't respond. The words lingered between them, heavy in the still air.

Then, as if realizing that this was not a conversation meant for the walls of the mosque, Usmanikka let it go. In that quiet moment, the weight of their shared concerns settled softly in the empty mosque.

Hamza extended his sturdy arms to help Usmanikka rise. A sharp twinge of pain shot through his back, but Hamza lowered his shoulder to support his weight, and together they left the mosque.

At his age, Usmanikka mused that he should be surrounded by children and grandchildren. Instead, his constant companion was Hamza—a man he once regarded as a stranger, but who had become like a son, though he had never openly said so. He believed Hamza was a virtuous young man, untainted by the vices that often troubled youth. There was a time when Hamza had secretly smoked cigarettes; Usmanikka had caught him in the act and given him a gentle tap on the head to put an end to it. Since then, he hadn't seen him smoke again, though he could never be entirely sure of any secret habits.

Usmanikka knew how swiftly one could be influenced in Dubai, for better or worse. The city, with its many places of worship, also offered easy access to liquor in upscale hotels. The thriving flesh trade underscored the city's dual nature. In Rigga and Karama, one could see Chinese and Russian prostitutes lined up for business— priced higher than the black, African women found on Frij Murar and Naif Road.

For a moment, Usmanikka wondered if such illicit pursuits might tempt Hamza, but he quickly dismissed the thought. He could not imagine Hamza, still young and a little inexperienced, falling into that life. He believed that with time, Hamza would grow wiser. Although he did not pay Hamza a regular salary, he always ensured that his sustenance was covered. In secret, he had been setting aside part of his earnings for a significant future event, perhaps even for Hamza's marriage.

As darkness fell over the mosque courtyard, a gentle breeze stirred. The end of summer was near, promising cooler days, though not as refreshing as they once were, with the city's growing concrete structures blocking the wind.

Hamza asked, "Ikka, you said you needed to go somewhere?" His tone held genuine curiosity as he sought to understand the destination.

"Ikka, are you really thinking of visiting that swindler again? And at Maghrib time?" Hamza pressed, his voice edged with disapproval.

Usmanikka barely glanced at him as he settled into the car. "There's something important I need to discuss with him," he replied.

Hamza started the engine, his face set in a frown. "Have you forgotten how he deceived you and stole lakhs of dirhams? And now you want to see him again?"

"Hamza, stop your commentary and do as I say. I already told you—I have an important matter with him."

The car began moving slowly. Leaning back, Usmanikka stretched his legs and whispered softly, "Ya Allah!"

Hamza's anger wasn't without reason; every word he spoke held truth. Usmanikka had come to know Muttalib when the latter worked as a salesman in a grocery store. Moved by compassion, Usmanikka had later employed him in his shop in Aweer, where he managed stock and collected revenue. Muttalib received a salary along with commission on sales, and Usmanikka had trusted him enough to let him oversee all the managerial responsibilities of the store.

At first, everything ran smoothly. But soon, profits began to fall, even though the stock levels remained steady. When questioned, Muttalib offered only vague explanations and excuses. It was Hamza who eventually discovered that Muttalib had been running his own grocery on the side, redirecting Usmanikka's goods to his personal store. As a result, Muttalib was dismissed. Some, including Hamza, even suggested handing him over to the authorities, yet Usmanikka chose to show clemency and pardon him.

As they parted, Usmanikka warned Muttalib to be watchful, so that his own staff would not betray him as he had been betrayed. After that incident, Usmanikka hardly gave him another thought. Still, Muttalib's treachery was not an isolated case; others had deceived him in similar ways. Usmanikka came to see money as a powerful temptress—a force that could drive people to act against their better judgment.

A week later, while at the vegetable market in Aweer, Usmanikka happened to see Muttalib again. The man looked defeated, his movements slow and labored. He had tried to avoid being seen, but Usmanikka caught his arm and asked how he was faring. Amid the curious stares of bystanders, Muttalib broke down in tears. "I've lost everything, Usmanikka. It's God's punishment for deceiving you," he sobbed.

Muttalib had been forced to close his store when many customers left without settling their debts. Wholesale suppliers had even taken legal action against him over unpaid bills, leaving him no choice but to sell his shop for a pittance—a move that only slightly lightened his burden and left him destitute.

When Muttalib blamed the economic crisis for his downfall, Usmanikka shook his head and corrected him, "No, this is not just about the crisis. It's the result of human frailty. Greed and avarice can overpower virtue. Many lose themselves in the pursuit of wealth, regardless of the cost."

Nevertheless, Usmanikka vowed to help Muttalib in any way he could. Memories of their shared past stirred deep compassion in him. Muttalib had wept, clasping his hands before Usmanikka and praying that God would reward his kindness.

After that meeting, Usmanikka was unable to see Muttalib again immediately. This delay made him worry that Muttalib might doubt his sincerity, thinking his assurances were mere formalities. In truth, Usmanikka's own finances had dwindled, and his savings were nearly gone. He was trying to gather enough funds during the week to help Muttalib settle his debts and reopen his store.

It was evening, and the roads were sparsely populated, allowing Hamza to drive at a relaxed pace. He remarked, "Look how our Dubai has changed. There is less congestion now, and many construction projects along the road have come to a halt."

"You are right, but hold on to your faith. Dubai will not crumble. I remain confident," Usmanikka assured.

"May it be so, Insha Allah!" Hamza expressed his hope.

"Insha Allah!" Usmanikka echoed.

Chapter 13

He logged onto the internet again and checked his bank account. A sinking feeling washed over him when he saw no new credit—the salary for the month had not arrived. It was already the thirteenth day, and his earnings for the previous month were still missing. Once, he had received his salary on the first of every month, but delays had become the norm. The due date had stretched to the fifth, and for the last two months, it hadn't come until the tenth. Now, even the thirteenth day passed without a deposit.

That morning, he had spoken with the accounts manager about urgent payments that needed settling as soon as his salary came in. The monthly apartment rent was his most pressing expense. Fortunately, the old practice of paying three months' rent in advance with post-dated cheques had been relaxed due to a fall in demand in Sharjah—a small relief in difficult times.

Beyond rent, he also had his children's school fees and overdue credit card payments to manage. Missing the minimum on his credit card meant incessant reminder calls from the bank—a prospect that filled him with dread. Utility bills for water and electricity were also looming; missing those payments could result in disconnection, and given the relentless heat even with the air conditioner on, he could not afford to lose these essential services.

He realized it had been a long time since he had shopped at major supermarkets like Lulu or Carrefour. His kitchen now lay nearly empty, and that scarcity forced him to reflect on his own situation.

Gopalakrishnan had shared all these concerns with the accounts manager, who listened silently. When he finally spoke, the Malayali accountant said, "You must be out of your mind to burden me with all this. I have my own troubles to deal with." He added, "My finances aren't any better than yours. Otherwise, why would I still be here at my desk in my sixties, despite all these age-related problems? These delayed salaries have thrown everything into chaos."

Gopalakrishnan asked, "Sir, do you have any idea when our salaries will be credited?"

"I can't say for certain. Let's wait for the Arbab to arrive; then we'll know. If he manages to arrange some funds, you might see your salary today. Otherwise, you'll just have to endure," the accountant replied.

Hours passed after the Arbab's arrival, yet Gopalakrishnan still saw no update in his bank account. It was clear the boss had been unable to secure the necessary funds. At that point, Gopalakrishnan decided he could wait no longer and needed to seek emergency credit on his own.

But he had no idea whom to turn to. He had already borrowed from two or three friends, and his credit cards were maxed out. Any further attempt to use them would likely be rejected.

Gopalakrishnan opened his drawer and searched his wallet. All that greeted him were a few crumpled notes that barely added up to a hundred dirhams. Tucked inside was a slip of paper—a grocery list that his wife, Padmavati, had prepared for the next day's meal. The list was sparse, covering only the essentials. "If I ignore this so-called 'home minister's' list, I'll have to go hungry," he thought.

He recalled the children's voices that morning as he dropped them off at school. He had promised to give them their school fees the next day, a promise that had left them visibly disappointed. His older son had warned that they might be left waiting outside the classroom if the fees weren't paid, while his younger insisted they would suffer under the scorching sun all day.

Their concerns struck him deeply. The irony of their suffering in a land famed for luxury stung him, and he often thought that his own homeland might have been kinder than this place where even basic needs came at such a steep price.

In the Gulf, many had once flourished on the wealth from petroleum, but now the recession had clouded the future. Those lured by promises of prosperity now faced the grim possibility of living in debt.

Just then, the office boy informed him that Arbab was looking for him. Gopalakrishnan made his way to Arbab's office and was surprised to see a softer expression on his boss's face. Normally, Arbab greeted him with a curt growl, but today he seemed more accommodating. Although Arbab was an Emirati citizen, he was originally an Iranian immigrant, and Gopalakrishnan had long noted that he treated others with less refinement and dignity than the native employers, who treated everyone equally regardless of their background.

"Dekho, abhi fax aaya. Yeh order bhi cancel ho gaya," Arbab said, showing Gopalakrishnan an invoice. Two days ago, the order had appeared nearly confirmed; the foreign company had even requested an invoice to finalize it. Now, they had withdrawn, blaming a lack of funds. In all likelihood, they had given the order to a competitor offering a much lower price.

The re-export business was in trouble because of the economic slump. Imported goods were piling up in warehouses, unable to be shipped out. Profit had become a thin margin between import and export prices, and some companies were forced to sell their accumulated stock at prices below cost. Many businesses in the Al Quoz area had simply vanished, leaving their intermediaries unpaid for their efforts.

Gopalakrishnan left the office a little earlier. He did not have enough money to shop at a large supermarket, so his only option was Moithukka's grocery store on the small road beside his apartment building. The store usually took orders by phone, delivering essentials like milk, yogurt, eggs, and pappadam right to his door. However, he never ordered the pricier items from there because Moithukka charged a premium. What might cost ten dirhams at a supermarket could run fifteen or even twenty at his local store.

Gopalakrishnan felt a small relief when he saw Moithukka alone in the store; the helper boy was nowhere in sight, and the lack of other customers eased the burden of having to ask for credit. It was a quiet humiliation, this need to beg for groceries—a well-dressed executive, driving his own car, reduced to that.

He explained, with a calm resignation, that he had simply forgotten to withdraw money from the bank. Moithukka, without a hint of suspicion, accepted the explanation, sparing him the discomfort of being told to fetch cash from the ATM at the nearby corner—a reminder of his diminishing dignity.

Yet, even after obtaining every item on Padmavati's list, her displeasure remained. She was a difficult person to satisfy, forever finding fault and, as he often noted, blaming him for even the oppressive heat. "I received a missed call from home," she said, her tone flat, as though the call carried the weight of endless grievances.

Gopalakrishnan looked at her, puzzled by why it mattered that she had received a missed call. Sensing his confusion, she explained, "It was your sister. The number was new, so I called back. She said you hadn't returned her calls, even though she'd been trying for two days. That's why she called me instead."

His temper flared. "Why didn't you tell her that your husband—yes, the man who somehow manages to stay alive—died two days ago, which is why he couldn't return the calls?" he retorted sharply.

Padmavati's eyes narrowed, and without another word, she left the room. Gopalakrishnan stood there, wondering why people back home couldn't simply pick up the phone and talk, instead of relying on these hollow "missed calls." Ironically, it was actually cheaper to call from home to the Gulf than the other way around—a fact that seemed lost on his homeland.

He had seen the missed call from his sister but deliberately refrained from calling back. He knew it was probably about the money he hadn't sent this month—a ritual he had never failed before. He wondered if anyone back home paid any attention to TV or newspapers. If they did, they'd know all too well about the recession, how jobs were vanishing, and people were returning home in droves.

He was waiting for his children's annual exams to end before sending his family home—keeping them together was becoming an impossible task under these conditions. His salary had been delayed for too long now, and a growing dread made him wonder if it would ever arrive. Alone, he might endure hunger and hardship, but the thought of his family suffering with him was unbearable.

He recalled speaking with Ashraf at the travel agency, insisting on reserving tickets for his wife and children. The Air India Express fares were the only affordable option, and he knew that if he waited any longer, those tickets would be snapped up by others sending their families home for the school vacation.

Clutching his mobile, he slipped out onto the balcony, careful to keep his conversation with Ashraf hidden from Padmavati's ears. She and the children had expressed a desire to stay, and he himself had doubts. Yet, he felt trapped; the rising number of suicides in the Gulf— stories of entire families ending their lives together under crushing debt—left him no choice but to consider sending them home.

On the balcony, a scorching wind did little to cool the sweat on his brow as he fumbled with his phone, struggling to reach Ashraf. The busy travel lines were a constant reminder that many others were caught in the same desperate race, and he cursed each moment as the connection failed.

Padmavati appeared at the balcony door, her tone teasing as she asked, "What are you doing out here? Checking out the ladies in the nearby flats?" Gopalakrishnan chuckled softly, appreciating her shrewdness. She stepped onto the balcony, her eyes drifting over the quiet street as if she expected to see something extraordinary.

Leaning in, he whispered, "If I can barely handle one, how could I possibly take care of another?" Her face fell into a slight sulk—a brief, knowing frown that only made him laugh again, the sound mingling with the cool, muted air of the evening.

Chapter 14

Nandakumar opened his laptop yet again and clicked through the online editions of Gulf News and Khaleej Times, searching for any position that might suit him. He had done the same earlier that morning, only to find nothing. Now, the pages offered no new leads, no fleeting hint of an opening.

He remembered a time, not so long ago, when countless companies had approached him with tempting salaries and appealing benefits. He had turned them away without a second thought, certain he already possessed the best offer in town. Now, with that job gone, any promising future felt elusive.

It made sense. Firms were not looking to expand. They were cutting back, downsizing, or slashing wages. Some had begun sending employees on indefinite leave, promising to recall them only when conditions improved.

It all began in the United States. Banks and financial institutions poured excessive funds into real estate and housing, offering vast sums without real security. Soon, supply outstripped demand, property values sank, and borrowers defaulted on loans they could not hope to repay. Seizing properties meant little, because auction sales yielded next to nothing. Eventually, banks collapsed, and institutions such as Lehman and Merrill Lynch fell too.

Obama's bailout did little to stem the tide, and the recession moved swiftly from America to Europe, and then to Japan, China, and elsewhere. Companies closed by the thousands, and joblessness spread like a contagion.

The Gulf region also reeled, hit hard by the steep drop in crude oil prices. Dubai, though not reliant on oil alone, still suffered because its principal income—tourism—began to wane as global travel slowed. Passengers at Dubai's airport dwindled, and hotel rooms stood eerily vacant, a silent testament to the downturn's unrelenting reach.

Another of Dubai's income streams lay in its construction industry, which featured countless freehold properties. Had the Central Bank not intervened, Dubai's fate might have been as dire as America's. The bank put a stop to fresh loans and demanded repayment of outstanding debts. A large share of investors turned out to be smugglers or those with hidden funds; once they pulled out, the construction sector froze.

Some of the major entities, felt the hardest blow. It held projects in foreign countries but, battered by the global crash, sold its overseas ventures for minimal sums and withdrew from international markets. At home in Dubai, their developments fell into disarray, leaving it deeply indebted to suppliers and contractors. Eventually, the companies opted to restructure and proposed a solution: half the owed amount would be settled immediately, while the rest took the form of a ten-year bond offering a ten-percent dividend.

More over the swift foresight of Rulers of Dubai and Abu Dhabi kept the nation from collapsing under the weight of recession.

Nandakumar sensed Sushama sliding onto the sofa beside him, though he pretended not to notice. His attention stayed fixed on the laptop screen.

She asked, "Aren't you going out anywhere today? You've been here since morning."

"No," he said tersely, then added, "If my being here bothers you, I can leave."

Sushama's face reflected disappointment. "Oh, no, that's not what I meant."

He offered a faint smile. "I didn't mean it either, dear."

She moved a little closer. "So, what's our plan? Are we leaving?"

He tilted his head. "Worried about losing Dubai's comforts, are you?"

Sushama looked flustered. "No, I was just asking."

Nandakumar let out a quick laugh. "Since when did you turn into the 'just asking' type?"

For a moment, Sushama grew quiet, and he observed the innocence in her expression. They had been married for two years, and she had lived with him in Dubai for that entire time, yet she still felt so hesitant about stepping outside her small sphere. She was college-educated, but lacked the confidence to move beyond her familiar routines.

Suddenly, the phone on the living room table started ringing, and Sushama rushed to answer it. She covered the mouthpiece with her hand and whispered, "It's Mother, calling from Abu Dhabi."

He realized right away that the conversation would last at least half an hour. She and her mother usually discussed every minor detail, and he ended up paying for that in the monthly telephone bill.

This time, however, Sushama returned sooner than he expected.

"That was quick," he remarked.

Sushama gave a small shrug. "Our phone bills are already high. I didn't want to chat for too long. There's no salary yet, so what else can I do?"

Nandakumar laughed again. "You silly thing—she was the one calling, which means your mother pays, not us."

Sushama blinked, looking almost sheepish. "Oh, that never crossed my mind!"

Nandakumar had always seen Sushama as strikingly innocent.

She said, "I've decided to cut down on expenses. Let's stop dining out and save whatever we can."

"Don't worry," he reassured her. "I'll find another job soon, maybe a better one. We have my savings in the meantime."

She looked at him, her voice firm. "Still, why waste money? You should be careful now. I've always told you not to spend recklessly."

He knew she was right. He had been extravagant for as long as he could remember—jetting off to new destinations at the slightest chance, never checking price tags, amassing every high-end gadget, stocking up on luxury cosmetics and designer clothes. For Sushama, too, he spared no expense. Birthdays and wedding anniversaries meant diamond jewelry without fail.

Only now did he face the outcome of those impulses. His talk of "savings" was a lie. Most of his money had gone into a plot of land in Kochi, and he still owed a significant amount to finalize that deal. On top of that, his monthly loan installments and mounting credit card bills weighed him down.

The lease on their Emirates Hill villa was almost up for renewal, and he knew the rent was too high. He couldn't imagine leaving that grand space for a modest flat. He wished he had saved a little more for moments like this.

Sushama studied his face. "Why do you look so nervous?" she asked with real concern.

Nandakumar paused, realizing she was still right beside him. He closed the laptop, pulled her close. She rested against his chest, and for a moment, he felt the weight in his mind lessen.

His cell phone rang on the coffee table, an unexpected jolt in the quiet room. He glanced at the screen and recognized the number as belonging to the British firm he had applied to. They wanted him to come in on Monday at ten in the morning.

Nandakumar pressed a hand to his chest, whispering a brief prayer. "Oh God, let this one work out. It's been so long since I've had a chance like this."

Sushama turned her head, concern in her eyes. "Nandetta, who was on the phone?"

He set the BlackBerry down gently. "A company wants me for an interview on Monday morning."

She brightened, her voice sure. "I know you will get this job. The gods will not ignore my prayers."

He leaned in and placed a kiss on her forehead. "Let your prayers be answered this time," he said, allowing himself a small thread of hope.

Chapter 15

It is widely acknowledged that whatever you urgently need has a way of eluding you, and no amount of searching can guarantee it will materialize when you want it most.

Johnny found himself in exactly that predicament. He had an important meeting with a prospective client, a sales inquiry that felt like the first beam of light in a long time, one that could lead to a substantial order. In the midst of a financial crisis, landing a major sale was more than a simple win; it promised to bolster his standing with management, possibly giving him a crucial edge against looming uncertainties.

Yet his car refused to cooperate. The engine would not start, most likely because the battery had run down. The vehicle was already overdue for servicing, a fact he had been ignoring while he dreamed of selling it and upgrading to a newer model. He had spent time in showrooms, evaluating different options. His friend Nandakumar, who knew cars inside and out, had walked him through every model's details.

Johnny's own budget for a new car was limited, but Nandakumar had assured him that he could get a bank loan for the full amount. He had good connections with the bank manager, who had offered favorable terms: a low interest rate and up to four years for repayment. That was before the financial crisis hit, shrinking Johnny's salary and shattering the entire plan. Now he worried about losing his job altogether, a fear that made the idea of a new car feel like a distant daydream.

Johnny felt uneasy when the company introduced sales targets alongside a salary cut. He dreaded the thought of losing his job in a sluggish economy, aware that securing even a handful of sales was difficult, let alone reaching those rigid goals.

Every client shared the same explanation: business was slow, and they might place orders once conditions improved. That vague promise left him frustrated.

When his car refused to start, he decided to take a taxi. As he waited under scorching mid day sun, memories of Dubai's earlier prosperity rose in his mind. He recalled a leader who propelled development with foresight, though some foreign residents had taken advantage of it. The city had opened property ownership to outsiders, hoping each person could settle into a flat or villa. A foreigner could sign a lease for ninety-nine years and pay in installments—a plan that once held the promise of broader opportunity.

Many of the buyers had hidden funds and questionable dealings. They took advantage of easy bank loans, planning to resell the properties at a profit. When banks tightened their rules after the overseas recession, those investors vanished, leaving buildings half-finished and silent.

Johnny stood on the sizzling pavement, nearly noon, sweat gathering at his collar. Fewer cars passed than before, yet every taxi he spotted carried passengers. The Roads and Transport Authority kept adding more taxis, though people still said it wasn't enough. He used to rely on his own car, so this wait felt like an unfamiliar test of patience.

He cursed his luck, sure the day was inauspicious. Time dragged on until a middle-aged driver pulled over, sporting a long white beard and kohl-lined eyes. He seemed like a Pathan, though slender rather than imposing.

Johnny gave him the address, and the driver answered with a quiet "Insha Allah!" During the ride, he explained how he once ran his own taxi, but a new rule banned private cabs. Now he worked for a company that demanded strict adherence to rules and daily quotas, even after eighteen-hour shifts.

Tourism was down, and many expatriates had left Dubai because of job losses, forcing drivers to endure slower business. This man supported his entire family back in Pakistan, but after deductions, his monthly earnings were meager. The crisis reached everyone, Johnny thought.

They merged onto Emirates Road, a route once teeming with cars when people chose it over the main highway to save time and avoid congestion. Even that stretch seemed quieter, another reminder of a city caught in the throes of change.

That had become a thing of the past now, and Emirates Road appeared noticeably less crowded. The slow lane on the far right remained nearly empty, though it had once been filled with trucks and containers. This shift arose from a decline in Dubai's import and re-export activities.

"Aap kya karte hain?" the driver asked Johnny. Johnny replied that he worked in marketing, and the driver posed a query similar to one Johnny himself had asked earlier: "Business kaisa hai aajkal, bhaisaab?" Ever since the recession began, people had been asking each other, "How are things?" and "Is there any hope?"

Johnny recalled a relative who had mortgaged his property back home before coming to Dubai in search of work. Soon after, the downturn cost him his job and drove him into severe distress. Eventually, he had to depend on others who pooled money to pay for his ticket home. Johnny imagined the heartbreak that must have greeted him upon his return, weighed down by mental strain when he had left for the Gulf with so much optimism.

Before long, Johnny's mind turned to another incident he knew. He remembered being jarred awake early one morning by a phone call from a close friend. The friend's hesitant tone conveyed a somber message that left Johnny unsettled, a reminder that these difficult times touched everyone in some way.

The news concerned a mutual friend who had endured a spell of unemployment in Dubai. Though he eventually found a job, the wages were modest. He managed for a time before deciding on a small business venture with a friend, supported by a bank loan. At first, the business looked promising, and he considered expanding it. Yet, when he reached the limit for bank loans, he turned to private lenders charging high interest, even pawning his passport. Tragically, his partner vanished with the funds, leaving him overwhelmed by debts.

The enterprise weakened over time and finally collapsed under the weight of the recession. Creditors began to threaten him, and the bank demanded repayment.

He also became ensnared in legal troubles when a cheque bounced. Johnny crossed paths with him one day in the bazaar, where he seemed deeply distressed.

Before long, the Police discovered his body on Jumeirah Beach. The details surrounding his death were unclear—some wondered if it was suicide, others thought a run-in with creditors might have led to his demise. Whatever the cause, his untimely passing had grave consequences for his family in his homeland, leaving them in a dire situation.

Suddenly, a thunderous crash hurled Johnny forward in his seat. The car jerked violently and slammed into a pickup van ahead, pushing it into the lane on the right and striking another car. The windscreen shattered.

The driver remained still, his head against the steering wheel. Johnny felt excruciating pain coursing through him and soon realized it was centered on his legs. He tried to move them but found them trapped in the crushed front of the car. Below his knees, his trousers were soaked, and blood streamed along his legs.

Police sirens wailed in the distance, growing louder with each passing moment. Traffic had ground to a halt because of the collision. Darkness seemed to close in on Johnny. Slowly, his senses faded until he could see and hear nothing. He lost consciousness and slumped onto his side.

Chapter 16

There were two people in the car: Althaf, who came from Kasaragod in Kerala and a Bangladeshi national. They waited patiently in the parking lot of Terminal of Dubai airport, having been informed that the Air India Express flight from Thiruvananthapuram had already landed. Passengers were now moving through immigration, and the individual they were expecting would appear at any moment.

By the exit gate stood a third person: Reji, from Kottayam. He was their leader, the one orchestrating the wait outside. He wore traditional Arab attire—a khantoora and an Agal—and was notorious in Dubai for doing anything, however unsavory, if the price was right. Adopting a fake identity, he called himself "Khamees Abdul Rahman" while waiting for Safiya, a thirty-year-old who believed she would be hired as a housemaid by an Arab household.

He knew he would recognize Safiya easily because the agent in Kerala had provided a photograph. He knew nothing about her temperament but was prepared for any scenario. If Safiya happened to be strong-willed and sensed foul play, she might make a scene. That was precisely why Reji wore the Arab robes, so she would mistake him for her genuine Arab sponsor, ready to take her directly to his home.

Reji addressed Safiya in a mixture of English and Hindi that she could follow, explaining that she was meant to work at his residence. All the while, he sized her up discreetly, confident that the money he had paid the agent was a good investment. At thirty, Safiya still looked quite attractive, with a sturdy frame and firm breasts. Reji considered her a promising asset, likely to yield considerable profit.

He collected her passport and visa before leading her to the car. Safiya felt a flicker of unease at finding two other men inside, but Althaf, seated at the wheel, calmed her by speaking to her in Malayalam and calling her "sister," telling her they would both be employed by the same Arab family.

Hearing Malayalam eased Safiya's worries. She slid into the back seat, where Reji settled beside her. In the front, next to Althaf, was the Bangladeshi, who turned to cast a look at Safiya. Then he exchanged a quick signal with Reji, confirming she was indeed the valuable asset they had expected. The car pulled out of the airport and made its way toward Reji's apartment in Frij Murar.

"From now on, she's staying here with me," Reji thought to himself. "Let the job and the Arab household go to hell."

Safiya's actual role would be worlds apart from what she had been led to believe. Reji planned to test her first, then hand her over to the Bangladeshi and Althaf. Some newcomers refused outright at the beginning, but Reji had no qualms about using violent methods if needed, and the Bangladeshi was disturbingly adept at such measures. Despite his short stature, he had a mean streak that could frighten even the toughest recruits.

Safiya, on the other hand, seemed to have come from a decent family, an unassuming soul who hadn't suspected Reji's intentions. The agent in Kerala had reported that she was driven by hardship, forced to leave her home because her opportunities were limited. Reji also knew she had borrowed money to fund her travel and pay the agent's fees. That same agent had pleaded with him not to make life any harder for her.

Reji let out a quiet chuckle. "No one ever built a thriving business by pitying other people's misfortunes," he mused. "I'm here for Dirham and an easy life. Everyone else's trouble is khalli walli!"

He wanted her to cooperate, to do as she was told, so he wouldn't have to get too rough. If she defied him, he'd have no problem resorting to force. Now that she was under his roof, the sensible choice was for her to comply and not even think of running. Above all, he wanted to recover the money he had paid the agent, then make a hefty profit off of her.

Seven women lived in Reji's apartment in Frij Murar, each from a different country. Originally, there had been two women from India, but one was dismissed when she contracted AIDS. Safiya's arrival brought the number of Indian women back to two.

Reji insisted on diversity in his "household" to cater to clients with varied preferences. Breaking in a new woman took time and effort. Those who quickly realized their situation and cooperated faced fewer hardships and earned more. Those who resisted were left without food or money. In the end, prolonged hunger wore them down. This was how Reji ran things.

While Althaf drove, he turned slightly and asked Safiya about her marital status. She told him her husband had passed away four years earlier, leaving her with two children in her mother's care. Althaf offered what he thought was reassurance: she could earn enough here to give her children a decent life if she committed fully to her job.

When they reached the apartment in Frij Murar, Safiya grew uneasy. "Why here?" she asked. "Shouldn't we go to the Arab's home?"

Althaf told her they needed to register her name in this building before continuing on. Moments later, they stepped inside, and Reji tore off his Agal and khantoora, tossing them aside. Safiya's eyes widened at the sight of him wearing only pajama bottoms. Reading the shock on her face, Reji laughed and spoke to her in Malayalam for the first time.

"From now on, this place is your home. Forget about that Arab family and that job you thought you came for."

Safiya's eyes darted toward Althaf, hoping he might help. Earlier, he had spoken kindly, even calling her sister. Now, he only joined in Reji's laughter. The Bangladeshi then spoke sharply in Bengali, and though Safiya did not understand his words, she sensed they were insults. She glanced at the door, thinking to run, but the Bangladeshi moved quickly to block her way.

Nearby, two doors creaked open under the racket in the hallway, revealing several women inside. Reji barked, "Back inside," and the doors shut again. Safiya cried out, pleading for them not to harm her and begging them to consider her their sister.

"Sister? We're guided by Dirhams, not such sentiments," Reji snarled. He shot a look at Althaf, who grabbed Safiya's arm. "Come with me," he said, pulling her into a room.

She struggled, and Althaf tightened his grip. "Now that you're here, obedience is the only way to stay safe and earn money. When they've made enough profit off you, they'll let you go. No one will ever know what happened."

Safiya sobbed, insisting she did not care about money, only her freedom. "I am a poor woman," she said, "a mother with two children who have no father."

At that, Althaf, who had seemed calmer until now, roared, "In the room, now! If you won't go on your own, we know how to make you."

The Bangladeshi moved in to help, shoving Safiya from behind while Althaf yanked her forward. Once they dragged her into the cramped bedroom, Reji took hold of her and flung her on the bed, ripping away her burqa with violent force.

Safiya's screams echoed off the walls as she fought with all her might, her desperation clear in every strained cry. Reji silenced her with a brutal slap across her face. While she reeled in pain, he tore away her simple maxi dress underneath the shredded burqa. He growled like a cornered animal and hurled himself upon her.

Behind them, the bedroom door slammed shut, and Althaf and the Bangladeshi erupted in coarse laughter, sounding unhinged. Safiya flailed her arms and legs in frantic resistance, her voice breaking with terror. But in a matter of moments, her strength gave out beneath Reji's overpowering force.

CHAPTER 17

Nandakumar arrived at Rashid Hospital shortly after Johnny was moved from the emergency room to the general ward. Unlike the overcrowded wards back home, where rows of rickety cots lined a single hall, this ward was divided into five curtained cubicles. Each cubicle contained a bed and a side table, along with a telephone, an oxygen mask, a nurse call bell, and other essentials.

The cleanliness surprised Nandakumar. There was no sharp odor of disinfectant, no chemical tang in the air. He couldn't help imagining how immaculate the special ward might be if the general ward was already this pristine.

It was Nandakumar's first time in a Dubai hospital. He had never been hospitalized himself, nor had he ever come to visit anyone. Whenever he felt unwell, Dr. Ali's clinic had always been enough.

The hospital staff had discovered Johnny's phone in his pocket while he was unconscious. Seeing Nandakumar's number at the top of the call list, they had phoned him, and he rushed over as soon as he heard the news.

Johnny was awake by the time Nandakumar arrived. He looked fine at first glance, except for the plaster cast around his right leg, which had multiple fractures, and the wound near his left heel.

Nandakumar took in the scene, troubled by how much had gone wrong all at once. He had lost his own job. Johnny was trying to manage on a reduced salary. Now, the accident. It felt like a deluge, he thought, one problem compounding another with no end in sight.

Johnny saw the salary reduction as an insult from his company, telling Nandakumar it clearly signaled they no longer valued him. He couldn't grasp how anyone could survive after such a sudden pay cut.

He had also remarked that businesses should simply dismiss unnecessary staff and hire fresh recruits at lower wages, so those let go could find jobs more suited to their needs.

Nandakumar had responded, "Johnny, remember this isn't our country. We're foreigners here. You should be glad to still have any work and the chance to earn a living."

Johnny forced a tired smile. "How did you find out about the accident?" he asked.

"They called me from the hospital," Nandakumar said.

Johnny gestured at the cast on his leg and the bandages around his other foot. "My bones feel crushed. Will I ever walk again?"

"Of course you will," Nandakumar reassured him. "They've treated the fractures. You'll be up in no time."

Yet Nandakumar's thoughts drifted to Johnny's family back home. He understood the weight of Johnny's worries and how quickly things could turn dire if he couldn't send them money.

A nurse came by then, administering what was likely a painkiller. Even in the face of heartbreak, Johnny tried to maintain a cheerful front, but Nandakumar sensed the effort it required.

Suddenly Johnny remembered the taxi driver. "Any news about him?" he asked. "He was a decent man. The accident happened while we were talking."

Nandakumar shrugged. "Might have been the distraction that caused it."

"No, it wasn't that," Johnny replied. "A pickup suddenly switched lanes and slammed on the brakes. We had no choice but to crash into it."

"Thank God you're alive, then."

Johnny's face clouded. "God? Does God even exist? What did I do to deserve all of this?"

Nandakumar glanced at him, voice gentle. "Only God knows His reasons. All we can do is trust there's some purpose behind what happens."

The nurse returned, checked Johnny's blood pressure, and recorded the reading. "Don't worry," she said with a kind smile. "He'll be all right."

She was Filipina, modest and polite. The hospital once employed many Malayali nurses, but patient complaints had prompted a shift toward hiring staff from the Philippines and Indonesia.

As the nurse was about to leave, Johnny asked, "Sister, how is the driver who came in with me?"

She hesitated for a moment before answering, "He didn't make it. There was internal bleeding. The doctors did everything they could, but..." Her voice trailed off.

A small, anguished sound escaped Johnny's lips. He remembered seeing the driver right before losing consciousness, his face resting on the steering wheel. It never occurred to him that it might be fatal. He figured the man must have sustained a severe blow to his chest or head. Johnny buried his face in the pillow, trying to muffle his grief.

Nandakumar quietly slipped out of the ward, worried about Johnny's expired medical insurance. The company had refused to renew it, suggesting instead that he handle it himself if he wanted coverage. The recession had touched everyone in different ways, Nandakumar reflected, and now he wondered how Johnny would pay his hospital bills. Maybe the taxi company would step in, but if not, Johnny would be left with a heavy financial burden.

"Hi, Nandu!" a voice called from behind. Turning, Nandakumar recognized Julie, the Goan woman who worked as a receptionist at his old company. He'd once found her attractive, but certain stories about her had made him cautious.

"My friend was admitted here after an accident," he explained.

She offered a playful smile. "My friend is here too."

Nandakumar felt the urge to leave, suspecting that continuing to talk with her could lead to a conversation he didn't want. Julie never seemed concerned about who might be listening, and she often spoke her mind without restraint.

He suspected she had been eyeing him for a while, given how often she suggested they grab dinner. At first, he hadn't taken those proposals seriously. Later, he learned it was part of her routine: she lured men in and took as much money from them as she could. She would even share a bed with them, provided they were generous spenders.

Just then, Nandakumar's phone rang. He fished it out of his pocket and saw a landline number he didn't recognize. A woman from a company he had applied to began peppering him with questions, although he had already included all those details in his résumé. He found it a little vexing, yet he answered calmly.

When she asked about his salary expectations, he mentioned the figure he had earned previously and explained that he wanted something similar. At once, she cut the call short.

Nandakumar wasn't interested in positions that offered less than he believed he deserved. Walking back to his car, he recalled the interview at the British firm, where he felt he had made a strong impression. British companies once paid quite well for the right talent, but he knew the recession had forced many to become more guarded with their budgets.

The British interviewer had seemed startled by Nandakumar's salary expectations. "But that's quite…," he began.

Nandakumar jumped in, "Yes, I think I shouldn't ask for more than that."

The interviewer gave a small laugh. "Let's see if we can fit that in…"

That interview had taken place days ago, and Nandakumar had heard nothing since. He presumed they had found someone willing to settle for a smaller paycheck.

As he unlocked his car, he realized he wasn't certain where to go next. He didn't feel like heading home; lately, Sushama's remarks had been getting under his skin. He thought about Lal Mirchi and decided to stop there for a couple of drinks. Seeing Johnny in such dire straits had left him drained, and he doubted he would sleep if he went straight home. He slid into the driver's seat, shut the door, and pointed the car toward Lal Mirchi.

Chapter 18

Standing at the edge of the creek behind the Hyatt Regency in Deira, with the surf thudding against the rocky embankment, Usmanikka appeared as unmoving as a statue. The tide rose and fell before him, and each crash of water mirrored a flood of memories in his mind.

He recalled his early days in Deira, back when he had first arrived by launch. He found work in Shindagha, known for its fish market, and Hamriya, famous for its vegetable market. Sometimes he unloaded produce from trucks and containers, other times he helped carry heavy fish baskets. There were stretches when he worked fifteen-hour days, and then sudden lulls with nothing to do. At that age, his energy seemed limitless, and he never felt weary.

Eventually, he became an assistant in a greengrocery, an experience that would later enable him to start his own store. He also peddled goods on Fridays at Sabka Bazar, laying them out on a large sheet for passersby: Sloan's Balm, Tiger Balm, Khojati Kohl, Jannatul Firdaus perfume. These were items travelers especially malayalis tucked away to carry home.

On Fridays, Sabka Bazar resembled a festive fairground teeming with people. Companies packed their laborers into pickups and brought them here to stock up on essentials and mingle with friends from their homeland.

After finishing their shopping, many people would treat themselves to a hearty meal in the neighborhood restaurants. Kadar Hotel was the most popular spot back then, practically the soul of Deira in those days. Usman recalled ordering tandoor roti, lentil curry, and king mackerel fry. Occasionally, he indulged in paya, a dish made from mutton legs.

Now, as he stood by the creek, memories flooded his mind in the same way the waves collided with the rocks. Hamza was leaning against the car, probably trying to figure out why on earth he had come straight here, in the semi-darkness right after dawn prayer, only to stand like a statue.

The truth was, even Usmanikka himself felt puzzled about his odd behavior of late. He chalked it up to something that might happen with old age, an unexplained urge to linger in certain places.

He signaled for Hamza to step closer. When the younger man approached, he grasped his shoulder and pulled him in. "Are you getting bored, waiting on me?" he asked.

Hamza's face had a tired look. "I really am," he admitted. "I was hoping to go back and get more sleep after the prayer. What's going on with you?"

"You fool," said Usmanikka, eyes fixed on the horizon. "You'd have to be my age to understand the satisfaction I get just standing here like this."

Hamza said, "Fine, enjoy your satisfaction. But remember, the Irani wholesaler will show up today to collect what you owe. Did you figure out how to settle it?"

"I spent the whole night trying to solve that," groaned Usmanikka. "Nothing came to mind."

"I've warned you repeatedly about giving your money away to every Tom, Dick, and Harry," Hamza scolded. "Now, none of them are around to help you when you're in trouble."

"I trust in God, Hamza. He will certainly help me."

"God?" Hamza's brows knit. "You think He has enough time to help everyone?"

"You're wrong. I've never done anything He would disapprove of. I've gone days without food but never stooped to anything sinful."

"Alright, but the sun's up now, and it's getting hotter. Let's leave before you catch a fever standing out here."

Once more, Usmanikka drew Hamza in and said, "You really are like a son to me."

Hamza felt pleased. "Well, then listen to your 'son.' Let's go," he said, guiding the older man back to the car. As they drove away, Usmanikka gestured to the open ground next to the Hyatt Regency.

"This was where people used to bet on wrestling matches every Friday evening. The wrestlers were Pathans, with bodies as solid as stone. I even tried my luck once, hoping to win some prize money if I managed to defeat my opponent. It was back when my Ernad blood was boiling, and in my very first match, I beat a Pathan."

Hamza broke into laughter. "You're making that up!"

"Yes, it's true," he went on. "But in the second match, another Pathan stepped forward and hurled me out of the ring. I was lucky my spine stayed in one piece."

For a while, Hamza drove in silence. At this early hour, Naif Road was still empty, the daily flow of school buses and company vans not yet in motion.

All at once, Hamza spoke. "Ikka, you seem troubled."

"Why do you say that?" asked Usmanikka, caught off guard.

"I can tell you're visiting these old places and reliving memories to chase away whatever sadness is weighing on you."

He didn't respond right away. He thought about how sharply Hamza had read him, discerning the churn in his mind. Indeed, he had been unsettled in recent days, though not so much by the slump in his businesses or the looming debts—he believed he could handle those. His worries ran deeper.

Even with Hamza by his side, he had felt loneliness creeping in, a longing to see his children and grandchildren. Yet he couldn't abandon his responsibilities in this fragile moment and fly back home. And his children, absorbed in their own lives, wouldn't come to Dubai even if he arranged visas and airtickets. The truth left him with an aching sense of isolation.

Hamza broke the silence, "Ikka, I never met my father. One day, as a kid, I begged my mother to tell me who he was. She broke down in tears and said she didn't know."

Shocked, Usmanikka turned to look at Hamza, who kept his eyes on the road. His face appeared tense, as though even recalling that memory made him uneasy.

"Don't dwell on it. Let go of the past," offered Usmanikka in a calming voice.

"I'm not upset, Ikka," Hamza continued, "but the moment she told me that, I left them both—my mother and my home. I haven't bothered to find out where she is since."

"That isn't right, my boy. She's still the woman who gave birth to you."

Hamza said nothing, and for a moment the car was heavy with unspoken thoughts. Watching him, it occurred to Usmanikka how each person carries a hidden storm, visible to none but themselves. Slowly, he reached out a trembling hand and set it on Hamza's shoulder.

Hamza's tears came suddenly. "I don't know who my real father is, but you have been more of a father to me than anyone else in this world."

"I've always thought of you as my son," answered Usmanikka softly, "dearer, in many ways, than my own children."

Chapter 19

When he finally managed to unlock the front door, Nandakumar heard Sushama's voice from the living room: "So this is the routine now, is it?"

Her tone startled him, and he turned to see her sitting on the sofa, the dim light casting shadows across her face. Usually, by the time he got home, she would have turned off the lights and gone to bed—though he knew she was never truly asleep, only pretending. He would often ignore that pretense and lie down beside her.

It was two in the morning. He had walked into Lal Mirchi intending to have two quick drinks and head home, but once there, he lost track of time. One or two drinks had stopped being enough, and he found himself returning later each night.

He wondered why she was still up. Was she waiting for him to confront him, or was there another reason? She used to call him on such nights, asking why he was late and when he would be back, until he scolded her for interrupting him with those questions. After that, her calls ceased.

Nandakumar cleared his throat. "You're not in bed yet?"

She shot back, "How could I sleep? How does a wife rest when her husband stays out past midnight?"

"Why the sudden concern today?" he asked. "You didn't seem bothered before."

"I decided it matters now," she said flatly. "How much longer am I supposed to put up with this?"

He kicked off his shoes, pulled off his shirt, and slung it over his shoulder, moving toward the bedroom in a swirl of anger. But Sushama jumped up from the sofa, blocking his path. "You're not walking away. Tell me, how much longer is this going to go on?"

Nandakumar's patience wavered. "What are you trying to do, starting a cross-examination at this hour?" he growled.

"If this is your plan, then yes," Sushama shot back. "I have to act."

"Are you threatening me now?" Nandakumar asked, anger creeping into his voice. "I can get worse, you know."

She gave a short, bitter laugh. "You've already become worse. Are you even the same Nandettan anymore?"

He felt a jolt of surprise at her sudden boldness. It puzzled him how she had changed so completely—she had once been docile, content to follow his lead.

In the same breath, he realized he had changed too. Ever since losing his job, he had become someone else entirely, the man who rarely spoke to her with affection. It had been too long since he had touched or held her with genuine warmth.

These days, he stumbled home late, intoxicated, and took out his frustrations on her in bed, as though punishing his fate. She lay there, unmoving, enduring it all. Often, he didn't even have the energy for it, leaving him feeling defeated. She stayed silent, gazing at the ceiling, then would gather her nightclothes and slip away to the bathroom.

Nandakumar let her angry words pass, aware they sprang from deep frustration. A late-night argument would only worsen things.

As he continued on to the bedroom, her voice trailed behind him. "Alright, you can share the bed with me," she called. "But don't you dare lay a hand on me."

Her comment provoked a sudden flash of anger in Nandakumar. "What if I do touch you?" he snapped.

Sushama let out a derisive laugh. "If only you showed this kind of passion in bed," she said.

He lost control. He lurched forward and slapped her hard, sending her sprawling on the floor. Then he raised his foot as though to stomp on her. "Shut up," he roared. "I've had enough, and you've pushed me too far. I'll kill you if I have to—remember that!"

She lay there, tears in her voice. "Go ahead," she said. "I'd rather die than keep facing your abuse."

Nandakumar snatched the damp shirt from his shoulder, balled it up, and flung it at her before turning toward the bedroom. Wheezing and drenched in sweat, he collapsed on the bed without bothering to change.

My God, it's come to this, he thought, trembling. *Harming my own wife.* His head felt hazy, his breath tight in his chest. He strained to hear any sound from the living room. A part of him wanted to go back and check on her, deeply regretting the blow he'd dealt.

He had never spoken to Sushama so harshly, let alone struck her. She'd always been a sheltered child, her parents' only daughter, quick to sulk when things didn't go her way. He'd never taken her tantrums seriously; they seemed like fleeting fits that would disappear in time.

Now, he lay wide awake, afraid she might do something drastic out of sheer humiliation. He'd heard stories about desperate choices women sometimes made, especially in these confined living conditions. The thought of it filled him with a deep, gnawing dread.

Suddenly, Nandakumar sprang from the bed and stumbled into the living room, feeling the liquor take hold of him more strongly than before. He could barely keep his balance.

He found Sushama still on the floor, her hand pressed against her cheek, tears streaming down her face. Nandakumar's heart twisted at the sight of how wretched he had made her feel. Crouching down next to her, he tried lifting her by the arm.

She shrank away, her voice trembling. "No. Don't touch me! I want nothing to do with you."

He spoke quietly, "Please don't say that. I'm sorry. I mean it."

"I'll leave in the morning," she cried. "My parents are waiting for me. They won't let me suffer like this."

Nandakumar tried to calm her. "Why cause them grief, Sushama? I've apologized. Why can't we let this pass?"

She shook her head, voice loud and unyielding. "I don't need your apologies."

Gathering himself, he wrapped his arms around her and pulled her tightly against his chest.

In a soft voice, he said the words she loved most, "Honey, I love you—truly, I do."

Her anger ebbed, and she rested her face against him, her sobs quieter now. Gently, he lifted her tear-stained face, pressing his lips to hers. Then, summoning every bit of strength left in him, he lifted the slight figure of Sushama off the floor and carried her into the bedroom.

Chapter 20

The young woman at the reception desk mentioned there was an urgent call waiting on the line.

Chandran Nair, sounding unenthusiastic, asked who was calling.

When she hesitated, he grew impatient. "I'm asking you who it is," he pressed.

She cleared her throat. "It's from the police station."

He clutched his chest in dismay. "Oh God," he muttered, "another call from the police."

Two days earlier, the Naif Police Station had phoned him about a post-dated check he had given to a building materials supplier. Normally, he bought his construction supplies on credit, paying off those bills as soon as his project invoices were settled.

Right now, two of his construction projects were stalled, and the money owed to him was still pending. In one case, the bank halted the owner's loan because the security was too weak; in the other, the owner had simply vanished, and his mobile stayed switched off.

Because of that, the check for the building materials bounced due to insufficient funds. Despite his long history with Chandran Nair's firm, the supplier couldn't extend the due date any further, even after he pleaded with them. They were feeling the recession's pinch too and had debts of their own, so they couldn't accommodate him.

With no funds to pay, he ended up with a police complaint against him. In the end, he managed to scrape together enough money from different sources and settled the bill at the station. It helped that the police inspector there had ties to his Arab sponsor—otherwise, he might have landed in jail.

And now, yet another call from the police station. Which check had bounced this time? he asked himself nervously.

The receptionist's tone turned impatient. "Sir, should I put the call through?"

Chandran Nair sighed. "Yes, go ahead and connect it."

A deep voice came over the line. "Are you Chandran Nair?"

"Yes, sir," he replied.

"This is the Muraqqabat Police Station. Could you come here right away?" The accent was crisp, the English polished.

"What is this about, sir?" Chandran Nair asked, but the caller hung up after saying, "I'll explain when you arrive."

He tried to get in touch with Sathyamurthy, his accountant, only to find he was out. Abdu, the office assistant, confirmed that Sathyamurthy had left. Calling his mobile got him nowhere; the phone rang endlessly without an answer. "He's never around when I really need him," Chandran Nair muttered. He wanted to check if they had any checks outstanding that might have bounced. Still, he knew there was no ready source of money to clear any shortfall. Credit in the market had dried up, and his bank accounts were nearly empty.

Deciding not to wait, he left the office at once, anxious to avoid the embarrassment of police officers showing up at his workplace. As he grabbed his car keys, he told the office secretary to contact the mandoob and ask him to meet him at the station. The mandoob, a Palestinian, would be invaluable as an Arabic speaker, given that Chandran Nair, despite years in the Gulf, never learned to converse in Arabic. He simply never needed it; English or Urdu was enough in Dubai, since many Arabs were fluent in both.

The inspector greeted him courteously. Chandran Nair handed over his business card, which the officer studied briefly before asking, "How is business these days?"

"It's tough, sir. We're going through a severe financial crunch."

The inspector nodded. "Yes, the recession has caused a great deal of trouble."

"Indeed," Chandran Nair said. "Most of our projects are either canceled or suspended."

The inspector gave a slight shrug. "I'm aware of the situation."

Chandran Nair felt his heart pounding, expecting to be presented with yet another bounced check.

He wondered how large it might be and worried about how he could possibly settle it with no funds at hand. He cursed Sathyamurthy under his breath for not returning his call—he needed the exact figures, or at least some warning of which checks were overdue.

The inspector rose from his desk and signaled for Chandran Nair to follow. "Come with me," he said.

They passed along a series of narrow corridors until reaching a cramped room where several young people stood in a line, their heads bowed. Two police officers flanked either side. The inspector asked Chandran Nair whether he recognized any of them. In the dim light, he scrutinized each face until one struck him—his son, Arun.

Pointing him out, Chandran Nair murmured, "That's my son."

Without permitting him to speak to Arun, the inspector said, "That's all I needed. Come with me," and led him away.

Chandran Nair's thoughts spun in confusion: why was his son here? He was all too aware that this emirate's laws were strict, with little chance of slipping through the legal net. Even the most skillful lawyer couldn't make serious charges just disappear.

Before Chandran Nair could ask any questions, the inspector explained the situation. The youths had been found at a villa in Khawaneej where, after cutting their classes, they threw a party. Normally, such gatherings wouldn't attract the police. This time, however, neighbor complaints about noise brought the officers to the scene, where they discovered not a typical celebration but an event awash in alcohol and drugs.

The inspector added that girls were present as well, though they were being held in a different room. "Because they were in a state of intoxication and had drugs in their possession, charges must be filed," he said. "The college authorities have been informed and will impose disciplinary measures. As your son's father and sponsor, you must now surrender both your passport and his. If bail is granted based on your plea, you'll be required to appear in court whenever summoned. If bail isn't granted, he'll remain in custody until the case is concluded."

Chandran Nair rose from his seat, feeling as though his entire body had lost its strength. On top of his financial struggles came yet another disaster. He imagined the shame he might face if people learned that his son, barely twenty, had been arrested for liquor and drugs. He wondered how his family here and his relatives back home would handle this grim piece of news.

The mandoob's call flashed on Chandran Nair's mobile, but he ignored it. He headed straight to his car, intending to drive home for both his and Arun's passports and return to the police station.

The phone rang again, this time showing Sathyamurthy's name. Nair answered with irritation. "Where have you been? You're never around when I need you. Why keep a phone if you won't pick up?"

Sathyamurthy stammered, "Sir, you asked me to see the bank manager again for the overdraft repayment extension. How could I answer when I was in the meeting?"

Chandran Nair remembered he had indeed told Murthy to speak to the bank manager. In the chaos, it had slipped his mind.

"Is there something else, Sir?" Murthy asked.

"The immediate crisis is over," Chandran Nair said. "But there's something else. Call our lawyer, Eesa Mubarak, and arrange an urgent appointment."

"What happened, Sir?" Murthy inquired.

Chandran Nair ended the call without replying.

He shut his eyes momentarily, leaning his head back against the seat. "Why am I facing all this?" he whispered to himself. "What did I do to deserve these trials?"

Chapter 21

They had taken a single room and split it into two cramped spaces using a flimsy plywood partition. Each half was tiny and stifling. A narrow window was sliced in two by the partition, though it let in no light because heavy curtains covered every inch of glass.

A single bulb dangled from the ceiling, but its switch was placed outside. The bulb remained off unless a customer came in, leaving the room in constant darkness otherwise. The bed took up most of the limited floor space. There was an air conditioner, but the partition reduced its effect, and it only ran for customers willing to pay extra.

Most of the men who visited were low-wage workers—people from construction sites, security guards, restaurant cleaners, and drivers. They had no money for the added air-conditioning charge and endured the sweltering heat for a fleeting moment of pleasure.

As a result, the room was hot and stifling, with barely any fresh air. An unpleasant smell lingered—a thick mix of sweat and semen, left behind by countless visitors.

Safiya was trapped in one half of that room, much like the others in the adjoining spaces. She was only permitted out for basic needs. Day and night, a steady flow of men kept arriving. On average, about thirty men a day came to that place, entering the two-by-two cubicles and the women's bodies forced to remain inside.

These men weren't just ordinary, Safiya thought; they were animals. She saw them as wild beasts that leapt upon her, devouring their fill without restraint. Their only aim seemed to be extracting every dirham's worth of what they had paid.

"Ya Rabbul aalameen…" she would whisper in the brief moments she managed to be alone. Even her prayers had to be muted here, in this place that denied her the freedom to weep aloud. Mostly, her tears stayed locked within.

Many people, including her mother, had warned her not to come to the Gulf. She paid them no mind, thinking only about her children's futures. They were growing fast, and she wanted to provide a decent life and a proper education for them. No other dreams had crossed her mind.

She believed that, even if it meant a struggle, she could reach those goals. Never had she guessed she would fall into this pit.

Jaleel had promised that she would work as a domestic helper for an Arab family—tasks she already knew from home, only with better pay. Two or three years of labor, he'd said, would give her enough savings to go back and live comfortably.

Her troubles began after her husband's death. Hunger became a frequent visitor, and hearing her children cry had cut her to the core. She resolved to take up whatever job she could find, despite warnings from relatives who claimed modest Muslim women shouldn't step out like that. They reminded her she was educated, and such work was beneath her, but her choice seemed unavoidable at the time.

Safiya's schooling had been possible thanks to her father's stable income. Her studies came to an end after he passed away. She recognized the value of education, yet she knew a tenth-grade certificate offered limited prospects in the world she faced.

She first encountered Jaleel at her workplace, where he would strike up seemingly casual conversations. At the outset, she mistook his interest for romance. Over time, she concluded his attention grew from pity. They became friends, sharing personal details. She confided in him about her hardships, and he insisted she deserved something better. Safiya, however, doubted she could find a better job.

Jaleel introduced her to the idea of working in the Gulf, describing a simple role caring for two children in an Arab household. Other chores, he promised, would be handled by other maids. He mentioned a salary of at least fifteen thousand rupees a month, which immediately tempted her.

Jaleel offered to handle everything for her and guided her to a travel agent who arranged the journey—though it came with a fee of thirty thousand rupees. The amount shocked Safiya, but she ultimately decided to proceed for the sake of her children's future. She mortgaged her house deed at the Co-operative Bank to get a loan, despite her mother's objections. In the end, she managed to convince her.

Until then, Safiya had rarely left her comfort zone in all her thirty-five years. Even once she started working, she went straight to her workplace and headed home afterward, paying little attention to anything else. She was devout, devoted to prayer, fasting, and keeping a path that pleased God. She never imagined how drastically her life might change.

A door creaked open—the inspection round had begun, as there were no customers at that moment. A week earlier, one of the women had escaped, breaking the confinement. Ever since, Reji and Althaf had been more vigilant and suspicious about the remaining captives.

The Bangladeshi, even more vicious than Reji or Althaf, specialized in breaking newcomers through deceit and brutality. Safiya was no exception.

On her first day, Reji forced himself on her soon after she arrived from the airport. She fought back with everything she had, but he overpowered her. Later that same night, the Bangladeshi, in a drunken rage, inflicted his own cruelty. He lashed her with a belt and starved her of food and water for three days.

When she still refused to give in, they resorted to an even harsher approach. The Bangladeshi pressed a burning-hot frying pan against her bare skin, beginning with her legs, then moving to her thighs and buttocks. She screamed as the metal scorched her flesh, but it meant nothing to him. He continued his assault, hissing like some crazed creature.

Eventually, as the scorching pan neared her breast, she broke down. In desperation, she begged Reji and

Althaf—who stood by, watching it all—to make him stop. "I'll do anything you want," she sobbed.

They translated her words into Hindi for the Bangladeshi, and he flung the frying pan aside. With a roar of satisfaction, he spat on her exposed skin, the red stain of paan masala running between her breasts.

The Bangladeshi demanded she lie with him right then. Despite the searing pain in her scorched thighs, legs, and buttocks, he showed no mercy. He unleashed his lust until he was satisfied. Althaf came next. He had once spoken kindly to her in Malayalam, but his cruelty rivaled the others'. Bastards, she cursed them silently.

Quite some time had passed since those first encounters, although she had lost track of the days. Time blurred into a repetitive cycle of day and night, with inadequate food, rest, or sleep. All she knew was that she had to share her body with whomever the Frij Murar or Naif Road agents sent in next.

She missed the life she had once known, where she bathed regularly and stayed ritually pure for her five daily prayers. Now, she remained perpetually unclean, passed from one stranger to another. It was impossible even to wash between visits, as the next customer would arrive the moment the previous one left. She saw around thirty men each day; on Fridays and holidays, the number rose to forty or more.

She was astonished at the variety of men who came to her. She had never realized how many types of individuals existed in the world. They were, after all, the same species—unlike the diverse beasts in a jungle, she thought—yet they sometimes seemed every bit as savage.

Safiya's heart pounded the moment the overhead bulb came on. Another stranger was about to enter, bringing with him his harsh appetites. She heard the door creak open and braced herself.

A man staggered in, clearly drunk, his body reeking of stale alcohol. Despite his unsteady stance, he showed no hesitation in his cruelty. For no apparent reason, he slapped her face and then covered her mouth to muffle her cries, nearly smothering her. It was all he required to satisfy whatever notion he had of manhood.

She had grown weary from imploring God so many times. Yet again, she cried out from within, "Ya Rabb, Most Beneficent, Most Merciful! Don't You see the plight of this wretched soul?"

Chapter 22

The hotel had once been Dubai's most celebrated five-star destination, its restaurant reservations fully booked on weekend nights. The nightclub throbbed with young men and women from every corner of the globe, moving in time to the beats a DJ spun through the small hours, their energy fueled by plentiful alcohol. Sometimes, Bollywood "item dancers" swept onto the floor, injecting even more spirit into the night. Everything operated under a proper Baladiyah license, so management never worried about surprise inspections, unlike many other clubs.

That evening, Adnan Firas walked in, fresh from recent trips to Hong Kong and Thailand. He'd gone there as a guide and translator for an Arab client who spoke no English, ensuring the client could navigate those unfamiliar countries. Adnan's consultancy served precisely these needs.

He was a regular at this nightclub. He saw it not only as a place to enjoy drinks and dancing but also as an ideal spot for making contacts and expanding his professional network.

When he first arrived in Dubai on a visitor's visa, he had little except his quick wits and a captivating charm. His tall frame and powerful build, combined with a talent for confident conversation, won over almost everyone. He remained courteous, even in the face of harsh treatment.

Before long, he had founded a general services consultancy in Dubai, fulfilling clients' varied requests—some of them morally questionable—provided the fee was right.

Tonight, however, the club took him by surprise. It was a weekend, but the usual crowd was missing, and only a smattering of patrons lingered inside. The DJ's music pounded through the speakers, yet the mood felt muted. Nine o'clock, the hour that ought to mark the prime of the evening, instead revealed a subdued atmosphere.

As he surveyed the nearly vacant club, Adnan realized the atmosphere would only grow duller as the night wore on. The ongoing recession had made people cautious, wary of spending in an uncertain job market. He felt its effects in his own business, too.

Unimpressed by the lackluster scene, he downed two drinks and decided to leave. The night was still young; he considered heading to a café for a Sheesha, but the idea felt uninspiring on his own.

He wandered into the hotel lobby and sank into a sofa. Out of habit, he pulled a cigarette from his pocket and placed it between his lips before remembering the no-smoking rule. Even here, usually a hub of travelers, only a trickle of guests passed by. Tourists were sparse, and Dubai's hotels, which relied on tourism and commerce, were feeling the pinch just as sharply as businesses that depended on oil in other parts of the Gulf. Many rooms remained empty, night after night.

The economic crisis had taken a toll on the stock market, with numerous companies seeing their share prices plummet. Adnan recalled how its shares once traded at sky-high prices. Some people had bought them with borrowed funds, but the downturn left them with crippling losses. Many fled the country, and others ended up in jail over bounced checks or missed credit card payments.

"Hi, Adnan!" a voice called, breaking into his thoughts. He turned to see Natasha, dressed in her flight attendant uniform, just back from the airport. He remembered that her airline provided rooms for its staff in this same hotel.

"Hi," Adnan replied, his tone subdued.

He and Natasha had dated once, back when she frequently came to his place at Discovery Gardens after finishing her shift, sleeping there until she needed to report for duty again. She always had a habit of asking for money, and besides showering her with expensive gifts and fancy dinners, he had given her substantial cash as well. He hadn't minded at the time; he truly loved her and had even considered marrying her.

But Natasha had other plans. She only wanted to siphon off as much money as possible until a better opportunity came along. The moment she got involved with a local Arab man, she stopped responding to Adnan's calls. He had been stung by her sudden indifference, especially considering the care and financial support he had poured into the relationship.

"Are you upset with me?" she asked, sensing his cool reception.

Adnan realized it was because he hadn't greeted her warmly. "Why should I be upset now? Our relationship ended a while ago," he answered.

Natasha tried to smooth things over. "Not at all, Adnan. How can it be over? Maybe you've forgotten me, but I haven't forgotten you."

Anger flared inside him. You little bitch, he thought. She's just angling to get back because that Arab must have left her. Otherwise, why show interest again?

"Anyway," she said, "let's not dwell on the past. Are you free for dinner, or do you have other plans?"

Adnan felt a sense of calculation. He believed the moment had come for retribution—for all the money he had spent and the hurt she had caused when she ran off with someone else. If there was one thing Adnan never forgot, it was a betrayal. And he tended to strike back at the first opportunity, delivering a harder blow in return.

"All right," Adnan said, "get ready quickly. We'll take a drive first, then find somewhere for dinner on the way."

Natasha agreed with enthusiasm, which to Adnan only confirmed that she wanted more money. Otherwise, why suddenly return and act friendly after ignoring him for so long?

Within minutes, she emerged looking gorgeous in jeans and a red top. Adnan felt a flash of temptation to spend the night with her at his place, but he pushed the idea aside. She was part of his past, a chapter he had no interest in revisiting. He had plenty of women in his orbit and saw no reason to take her back now that she was done with her other options.

He resolved instead to focus on his plan to make her pay for what she had done to him. This was a perfect chance, and he wouldn't let it slip away. The only question was how to execute his revenge. Physically harming her would risk a police complaint. Not even his best connections could protect him if he faced serious charges. He wanted retribution without endangering himself.

Natasha, an Armenian educated in the UK, worked as a flight attendant, helped in large part by her fluent English and striking looks. Adnan had met her at a nightclub, casually asked for her number, and called her two days later. After a few dinners out, she had started spending the night with him as well.

They drove through quiet streets, Natasha switching on the stereo. An Arabic song drifted out from the FM station. She didn't bother changing it, just leaned back and tapped her fingers in time to the melody.

All the while, Adnan's mind whirled with possible ways to get even with her. He had to be careful—any overt violence could land him in legal trouble, and he refused to risk his own safety or freedom. Still, he was determined to teach her a lesson.

Suddenly, Natasha's voice broke into his thoughts. "Where are we going, Adnan? We're a long way out of the city." He realized they were barreling down Al Ain Road, beyond the urban limits. The highway lay empty under the night sky, not another car in sight.

Adnan abruptly threw a question at Natasha: "Tell me, why did you abandon me? I gave you everything you asked for, yet you still left. I want an answer now."

The suddenness of it made her flinch. "No, I didn't abandon you," she said nervously. "I just got caught up with things. It became hard to see you."

"This bitch is playing her little game all over again," Adnan thought, his fury mounting.

Natasha went on, "How could I forget you? I'm still in love with you, I swear."

"Yeah, I love you too, but in a different way. Now, watch this," Adnan shouted, his own voice sounding strange to his ears. He wrenched the steering wheel, steering the four-wheel drive into the dunes by the side of the highway. Once he'd brought the car to a halt in the sand, he got out and yanked Natasha from the passenger seat. She fell forward, her face hitting the sand with a dull thud.

His rage boiled over. He climbed back behind the wheel, sending the vehicle roaring forward and then circling around. Natasha struggled to stand, confusion etched on her face, when Adnan hit the accelerator, driving straight at her at high speed. He ran her over—more than once—his tires flinging sand into the air each time they rolled across her body.

Chapter 23

Rashid Khalifa was at a Starbucks in Dubai Mall, flipping through the local section of the Khaleej Times. He muttered under his breath, "She deserved it, no question about it." Across from him sat Nabeel Hassan.

"What's going on, Rashid?" Nabeel asked.

A cruel smile took shape on Rashid's lips. "You remember that air hostess, Natasha? Back when you first saw us together, you told me to break it off. This news story concerns her."

Nabeel frowned. "What happened?"

Rashid gave another satisfied smile. "Someone killed her by running her over with a car. They found her body in the dunes off Al Ain Road."

Nabeel grunted, nothing more. Rashid had assumed Nabeel might show a bit more reaction, since Nabeel had been the one who warned him, back when he first saw Rashid and Natasha together. After all, they weren't just childhood friends; they were business partners, and Nabeel genuinely worried about him.

Initially, Nabeel cautioned, "You have a wife and child. How do you think they'll feel if they find out about this affair?"

Rashid dismissed the concern. "My wife wouldn't care if she did know. She's too busy with her spa treatments, fancy abayas, and running around in her Mercedes."

Even with Nabeel's persistent warnings, Rashid kept seeing Natasha. At one point, Nabeel noticed him withdrawing unusually large sums from their joint company account. It led to arguments.

"How can we move forward as a business if you do that?" Nabeel demanded. "We agreed on limits for partner withdrawals. So why did you violate it?"

Rashid responded coolly, "I had an urgent need. If it bothers you, I'll arrange the money and deposit it back."

Nabeel spoke in a bitter tone. "Rashid, this isn't about the money itself. Why are you withdrawing such large sums without telling me?"

"You don't need to know everything I do," Rashid said. "It's personal."

Nabeel smiled sympathetically. "Maybe you won't share the details, but I already know where your money goes. If you want to call it personal, I won't push. Just remember: you'll regret it eventually."

Nabeel's warning proved true soon enough. Despite the extravagant gifts and blank checks Rashid gave her, Natasha ultimately left, taking everything she could in the process. He had even traveled to various countries under the guise of business trips, meeting her during her flight layovers. Now, as Nabeel predicted, Rashid felt the weight of regret.

They had grown up together in Satwa, attending the same school. Both were bright students who earned scholarships to study business management in America. On returning, they launched their own venture with grants from the Ruler's office, meant to support young entrepreneurs.

In the beginning, the company flourished, with consistent profits in each deal. They began in a small flat, then expanded into a towering office in Dubai Marina, ultimately employing sixty people. Their success was something to envy.

Then the economic crisis struck. Rashid believed that his affair with Natasha played a part in their downfall too. Now, their business owed hefty debts, while the amounts owed to them were minimal by comparison.

Nabeel asked Rashid to discuss the company's future in a quiet spot away from the office, where they could avoid phone calls and constant interruptions. He suggested Dubai Mall, and Rashid agreed.

That was how Rashid ended up at the café, flipping through the Khaleej Times when the news about Natasha caught his eye.

"Natasha! Let her go to hell," Rashid thought to himself.

Nabeel put down his coffee mug and said, "We need to decide on a new plan. If we keep going like this, we'll just end up in bigger trouble."

Rashid nodded, though he was at a loss for what to do next. They needed a fresh infusion of equity to revive the company, but there seemed no way to get it. Banks wouldn't lend more to a business already drowning in debt, and government support wasn't an option.

They were already late paying the previous month's salaries, and now it was well into the next month. Rashid knew how badly this would affect employee morale—most staff were expatriates who had families back home relying on their earnings. The longer the delay, the more restless and disinterested they'd become.

On top of that, if anyone took their complaint to the labor office, it wouldn't be as easy to talk their way out of it as it might have been in the past. The authorities had begun emphasizing equality and justice, even for local Arab businesses.

"Why don't we shut down our major operations for a while?" Nabeel proposed. "We could keep a skeleton office going so they won't cancel our license."

"What happens to the staff?" Rashid asked.

"They'd take a break and come back once we're ready to operate fully again."

Rashid shook his head. "That will only make things worse. Creditors won't allow further delays, and our debtors will vanish if they think we're not active."

Nabeel fell silent, trying to weigh the options.

Rashid found himself drifting into recollections of simpler times. He and Nabeel both had grown up in humble conditions, satisfied with small-scale living and free of big ambitions. Their families earned a modest income through traditional work, without greed or aspiration for luxury.

Yet, over time, everything changed. People no longer wanted small houses; they wanted sprawling villas with multiple cars, household help, and the latest gadgets. The discovery of oil in the Gulf brought wealth on a grand scale. Couples lived in large homes where they might go for days without seeing each other: the husband off to work at dawn, the wife dressed up for her daily shopping, and children raised by maids—losing the close bonds that once held families together.

It wasn't just Gulf citizens, either. Rashid knew foreigners in the Gulf whose lifestyles had changed in similar ways. Family conflicts escalated, and divorce rates rose, affecting people of all backgrounds.

Nabeel's voice brought Rashid back to the moment. "What are you thinking about?"

"I'm considering selling my Abu's villa," Rashid replied. "It was granted by the government in his name, but since he's listed as the owner, we can sell it if we want."

Nabeel looked shocked. "Are you serious? Will your Abu agree to that? It was given to him when he retired. Where would he live?"

Rashid shrugged. "I'm his favorite. He'll understand. For a while, he can stay at my villa."

Nabeel frowned. "What about your wife? Will she welcome him?"

Rashid let out a short laugh. "Don't be naïve. He won't be in the main house. The old Majlis outside is empty anyway, ever since I built my new villa."

Nabeel hesitated. "That seems harsh. He's your father, and he sacrificed a lot to raise you…"

Rashid waved him off. "We need capital, Nabeel. That's what matters right now. I can't think of anything else."

Rashid's phone rang, cutting short their discussion. Irritated, he answered, "What is it? I told you not to call me today."

The secretary's voice quivered. "Sir, it's urgent."

"What kind of urgent?" he snapped.

"Sir, the police are here. They want to speak with you."

He stiffened. "The police? About what?"

In the next breath, another voice came on the line—clearly belonging to an officer who must have taken the receiver. "We need you at police headquarters for questioning regarding the air hostess Natasha's murder."

Rashid's mind raced. "I had no connection with her anymore. We used to meet, yes, but I haven't seen her for a long time."

"Still, we need to confirm," the officer said, his tone almost amused. "Your name's in her phone contacts. We also found some messages from you—some of them threatening. Don't you agree we should talk to you, Rashid?"

He sagged in his chair, feeling hollow. "Damn it," he muttered under his breath. "Bitch has come back to haunt me, even after death."

Chapter 24

As soon as they returned to the villa with medicine after visiting the doctor, Hamza turned to Usmanikka. "In times like this," he asked, "why do you never think about going back to your family?"

Settling onto the bed, surprised by the question, Usmanikka glanced at Hamza, trying to read his expression, but saw nothing there.

Hamza removed the boxes of medicine from the pharmacy bag and lined them up on the table. Then he went to the kitchen, boiled water in the kettle, and brought back a glass of hot water.

Accepting it, Usmanikka asked, "Hamza, are you tired of me?"

Hamza looked momentarily uncomfortable. "What are you talking about, Ikka? How could I ever be tired of you?"

"Then why keep asking why I haven't gone back home?" said Usmanikka.

Hamza hesitated for a second before continuing. "It's just… at your age, you should be among your family. You have everyone there, while here you're alone, your health so fragile. If something happened to you…"

"You mean my death?" asked Usmanikka with a dry smile.

"No, not that," Hamza stammered. "I'm just saying we have to be careful."

Pulling the blanket up from where it lay crumpled at his feet, Usmanikka covered himself. The air conditioner was off, yet he shivered. His fever lingered, and the doctor had pointed out fluid in his lungs. He had warned that if he'd delayed coming in, it could have turned into pneumonia. Fortunately, it wasn't that severe yet.

Despite his age, and aware of his fragile condition, with high blood sugar, hypertension, and an erratic heartbeat, Usmanikka often neglected his prescribed medications. He'd see the doctor, collect his pills, then stop taking them after a day or two. Hamza urged him to be more consistent, but he always found excuses.

He also knew Hamza's concern about returning to his family wasn't only about his health. Hamza understood him well, having shared the same roof and daily routines.

Business had been sluggish for a while, and he struggled to make a profit. He had to sell off the Meena Bazar café and the Aweer grocery store, hoping to cut further losses. He also sold the laundry to the Bihari tenant who previously leased it, accepting a minimal price. His remaining ventures were losing money, and he was running low on funds just to cover daily expenses.

He thought about how people in similar small businesses usually safeguarded their future by investing back home, building projects for a steady income in old age. They wouldn't have to depend on anyone.

He regretted not doing the same. Most of what he earned had gone to his children and grandchildren, or to anyone in need who crossed his path. Now, he wished he had been wiser. Still, it was no use lamenting the past.

He watched as Hamza walked to the kitchen again. In a few minutes, Hamza returned carrying a steaming bowl of gruel, placing it on the table beside him. Then he said, "Ikka, I'm going out for a bit. I might track down some of those layabouts who owe you money and see if they'll pay."

"Don't pressure them," cautioned Usmanikka. "Don't argue. Take the money only if they hand it over willingly."

Hamza let out a laugh. "You must be joking, Ikka. Do you think there's anyone in the world who'll happily return borrowed money without a fuss?"

"Hamza, you know everyone's tight on funds these days," replied Usmanikka. "That's just how things are in Dubai right now."

Hamza laughed again. "You gave money to anyone who asked, and now you can't even afford your medication. Yet you insist we shouldn't press people for what they owe. Maybe I should give them a friendly kiss on the cheek and politely ask for it?"

At that, a loud guffaw escaped from deep within Usmanikka.

As Hamza opened the door to leave, he heard the familiar call behind him: "Drive carefully!" He was used to that warning every time he started the car's engine. Sometimes, the caution annoyed him enough to snap back, "I'm a skilled driver, Ikka. I wouldn't have a valid license otherwise." But still, the older man persisted in reminding him to be safe.

While eating the gruel Hamza had prepared, a stray thought passed through Usmanikka's mind about going home for a while—maybe seeking treatment and regaining his health before coming back. Then he remembered he had nowhere to stay. The house he once stayed with his wife was now in his youngest daughter's name. After his wife passed, that daughter had insisted she deserved a home of her own, especially since he had helped his other children financially when they bought their houses. He had reluctantly agreed to sign it over.

He'd have to stay with that youngest daughter, but he was uneasy about the idea. After she got the house, she'd grown distant, barely speaking when he called. He doubted she'd truly welcome him, and even if she did, he feared she would tire of his presence in a matter of days.

He felt the same about his other children too. None seemed interested in him, not now that there was nothing to gain.

Most who came to this desert land planned to save money and hurry home, viewing it as temporary, like a lodging they'd eventually leave behind. But for him, it was different. He'd spent just eighteen years in his homeland and more than fifty here. He couldn't call this place foreign, no matter what anyone said; to him, it was home. He intended to be buried here when his time came. Until then, he wanted nothing more than to stay, counting down the days until Allah decided otherwise.

He had told Hamza as much, who always teased, "So you're determined not to leave, even in death?"

When he finished the bowl of gruel, he phoned his youngest daughter. She picked up promptly but became cool and curt the moment she realized it was him.

He ended that call and tried his eldest son next, but no luck—unreachable. Then he dialed his younger son, and after the usual greetings, he told him about his health, half-hoping the boy would urge him to come home. Instead, the younger son suggested he stay put, insisting Dubai's medical facilities were far superior.

Sighing, he decided not to call his other children. He could guess what they'd say.

A man pushed the door open and stepped into Usmanikka's room. Recognizing him as an old acquaintance, Usmanikka sat up on the bed, greeting him with a nod. The man was a commission agent, here to ask about his businesses. He offered to scout out buyers if he intended to sell.

"It's true, I sold a couple of my shops," said Usmanikka, "but if I sell everything, what will be left for me to do here?"

In a hesitant voice, the agent said, "Hamza mentioned you might want to sell it all and go home."

"No." A firm note entered his voice. "Where would I even go? This is my country. I know things are difficult now—worldwide, in fact. But just wait. A year or two, and Dubai will rise again, better than before. I'm sure of it."

Disappointment plain on his face, the agent left. Frustration flickered in Usmanikka's eyes, and he clenched his teeth. "Hamza, that hamk. Let him come back, and I'll have words for him! When did I ever say I was going to sell everything?"

His reaction to the agent stemmed from the belief he had just voiced: his unwavering faith in Dubai. "This city might stumble," he thought, "but it will never truly fall. Hundreds of thousands depend on it for their income. God won't ignore those prayers. Dubai will bounce back, stronger than ever. I know it."

Chapter 25

Nandakumar couldn't forget it was December 31 as he drove back from the airport. He had just said goodbye to Johnny, who was returning home. The year 2008, which had been a nightmare for Nandakumar, was coming to an end, and at midnight, a new one would begin. 2009. He wondered what lay ahead for him.

The recession had cast a shadow on the usual holiday celebrations. Official orders had discouraged the grand festivities that typically took over hotels this time of year, urging people to show restraint. Even so, he felt a quiet admiration for Dubai's ruler and the measures taken to keep the economy stable. While great powers like America were stumbling, this small country had managed to keep its banking system strong.

They had wisely scaled down or paused non-essential projects, limiting unnecessary expenditures. Companies though seemingly weakened, had settled its debts with creditors. Share values were inching upward again. India, too, had acted quickly: the Reserve Bank intervened to safeguard institutions before they could topple. The early nationalization of banks had paved the way for these rescue measures.

In past years, Dubai would be buzzing on New Year's Eve, with lively hotel parties, neon-lit streets, and big mall galas. Friends and families gathered at home to welcome the coming year, and at the stroke of midnight, fireworks blazed across the sky.

Ordinarily, Nandakumar and Johnny would have spent New Year's Eve at a posh hotel lounge, drinking and dancing until midnight. When the clock hit twelve, the lights would dim, everyone would share greetings, and they'd cut a celebratory cake before dinner.

This year, however, there were no gatherings or lavish parties. Nandakumar was, in fact, relieved. With his life in shambles—his lost job and his recent estrangement from his wife—he had no capacity to revel.

He and Sushama had briefly reconciled the night he came home drunk and violent. He believed all was forgiven. But in the morning, she attacked him again with criticisms, refusing to let the argument go. His efforts to avoid a fight failed, and her barrage of insults pushed him over the edge, leading him to strike her again.

Her subsequent behavior made it clear that she had been waiting for just such a moment to leave. She cried, called her mother in Abu Dhabi, and recounted the entire story. Her parents were the type who never stopped meddling, even after their children were grown and married, constantly offering "guidance." Sushama had always heeded their words more than her husband's. Rather than calming matters, they fanned the flames. They arrived soon after and took Sushama away to Abu Dhabi without asking Nandakumar's permission.

As they left, Sushama's father offered his opinion: "It's best if the two of you live apart for a while and sort things out. Otherwise, this will only escalate."

So Nandakumar found himself alone. At first, he actually welcomed the idea, thinking some peace might do him good. He relished the freedom for a few days—sleeping and waking on his own schedule, wearing whatever he pleased. He came home well past midnight, half-drunk, and fell asleep on the sofa, still in his clothes.

Had Sushama been around, she wouldn't have let him be so careless. She would have roused him, pressed his clothes for the day, set out his breakfast. She would have seen him off from the veranda, with a wave and a smile. He used to bristle at her controlling ways, but now, he missed them. The brief sense of relief in his empty house was replaced by a hollow loneliness. At times, he thought he heard "Nandetta…" echoing through empty rooms.

Seeking solace, he turned to alcohol more frequently, even drinking at home. Yet the numbing effect was never enough to rid him of his gloom.

He'd always confided in Johnny, but now Johnny lay bedridden. There had only been two people he trusted enough to share his thoughts with—Sushama and Johnny. And at the moment, he had neither.

Johnny had stayed in Dubai for a while, undergoing treatment, but when he failed to improve much, they decided he should continue treatment back home. His condition was so bad that when Nandakumar accompanied him to the airport, Johnny had to use a wheelchair to board the plane.

Seeing him that way was heartbreaking. The once-strong Johnny now appeared painfully thin, nearly unrecognizable. Because his company hadn't renewed his medical insurance, he was stuck paying huge medical bills.

He borrowed money wherever he could. The accident insurance payout would only come after the legal process ran its course, and he'd already hired a lawyer before leaving. As if that wasn't enough, the company didn't even cover his flight ticket, taking the cost out of a prior loan they said he owed.

Nandakumar wondered how Johnny would manage further treatment back in his home country without having to borrow again. He pictured Johnny returning to his family—after long years in the Gulf—empty-handed and in a wheelchair, and he could only imagine the sorrow of the family who had depended on him for so long.

Nandakumar couldn't help him, either. He had lost his own steady income, and the savings he had left were minuscule. On his way back, he decided to stop at the nearest petrol station, with his tank nearly empty. It struck him how, at this time last year, stations had been jammed with cars as people flocked to Dubai for the holiday. Today, it felt like another sign of how much had changed.

Dubai was famous for its many attractions: Burj Al Arab, the tallest hotel; Burj Khalifa, the tallest tower; and Atlantis on the man-made Palm Jumeirah. Then there were the endless parks, malls, beaches, and theaters. Yet on this New Year's Eve, few visitors had come to the city. Nandakumar noticed hardly any cars at the fuel station or on the roads near the airport. The streets felt deserted, and he recalled the dusty cars in the airport's parking lot, likely abandoned by people who had left for home, unable to repay their vehicle loans.

His phone rang, and he saw it was Johnny, calling from the airport. He had cleared the checks and was waiting for his flight. Johnny said quietly, "Nandakumar, this is all so unfair. You lost your job, and I'm almost helpless now."

Nandakumar tried to reassure him. "Don't let it get you down. It's New Year's Eve. Maybe the new year will be kinder to us."

"All right, Nanda," Johnny said. "I'll call once I'm home."

After he finished refueling, Nandakumar decided to park and grab dinner at the food court. His refrigerator at home was empty, and he'd been cooking more lately, not only to save money but because restaurant meals had been upsetting his stomach. Tonight, though, it was too late for grocery shopping and too late to prepare anything. Eating out would have to do.

McDonald's at the food court bustled with activity. Nandakumar noted that no matter how severe the crisis, fast-food places and grocery stores always seemed to draw crowds—everyone had to eat, after all.

After he bought a burger and a cola, he scanned the seating area and spotted Arshad in a corner. To his surprise, a Filipina woman sat beside him, both of them chatting animatedly over their meals.

Arshad came from the same hometown as Nandakumar and worked at an advertising agency in Dubai. They'd run into each other often. Arshad's father was a Moulavi back home, a highly respected figure in their community. Nandakumar felt a pang of concern at the thought of the Moulavi discovering his son in close company with a Filipina—especially since Arshad was already married, presumably with children.

He remembered stories of Filipina women charming young men into lavish spending. Sometimes they brought friends, and the man would foot all the bills. In return, he might receive a kiss or, if lucky, spend a night together. Eventually, the money ran out, credit cards went overdue, and legal troubles ensued. By then, the woman would have moved on.

Deciding it would be best not to embarrass Arshad, Nandakumar selected a table away from them. Perhaps this was Arshad's method of coping with his own burdens, Nandakumar thought, and he saw no reason to intrude on his privacy.

Chapter 26

Special occasions were always marked with gusto in the bachelor quarters. During festivals like Onam, Vishu, Eid, or Christmas, they threw big parties, let the booze flow, and danced around with zero reservations. Some passed the time with cards or a lively round of carrom, determined to make the day memorable.

This particular bachelor room was no different. Preparations were well underway for New Year's celebrations. Eight men from Kerala, varying in age and faith, shared this space. Despite the room's modest setup, they managed to live in relative harmony, each one helping the other whenever problems arose.

There was one unwritten rule: only Malayalis could live there. If someone left for good, the bed stayed empty until another Malayali showed up to fill it.

Nasar and Jose entered carrying a bottle of liquor they had gotten from Umm al Quwain. They had driven back nervously, worried the Shurtah might stop them. In Dubai, purchasing alcohol required a permit, but Umm al Quwain had looser regulations, letting them buy as much as they wanted.

They had picked a brand high in alcoholic content, tailor-made for their New Year's party. Nasar didn't drink—it was haram for him—but he urged the others to indulge all the more. Jose, on the other hand, was a seasoned drinker who usually lost what little control he had once he was drunk.

Aravindan was in charge of getting the cake, and he arrived right on schedule with a Black Forest cake he had ordered from Caesars two days before. Meanwhile, "Ikka," known as Mujibukka, would handle the cooking, assisted by Mansoor, the newest member of the group.

There were rumors among the roommates that the bond between Mansoor and Mujibukka ran deeper than mere friendship. After all, when someone spent two or three years away from wife they might seek comfort in whatever companionship was available. Whether that applied to these two remained unclear.

They shared the room with three other men. One was away on a family vacation, and the other two worked as security guards, not expected back until late at night.

Jose popped open the bottle. Nasar, who abstained, observed, "Things are looking bad. I've been in Dubai for eight years, and this is the first time I've seen such a quiet New Year's Eve."

"People have no money to spare for partying," Jose replied, pouring out the liquor. "And those who still do are hanging on to it in these times."

From the kitchen, Mujibukka leaned out. "Drink as you like," he pleaded, "just don't start a fight like you usually do."

Aravindan, never shy about expressing an opinion, declared, "What's the point of drinking if there's no fight to go with it, dear Ikka?"

"Don't put on a show," Ikka teased him. "When fists start flying, you're the one who dashes off to the bathroom, pretending nature calls."

Their laughter was cut short by the doorbell. Standing outside were Menon Sir, who lived in the adjacent flat with his large family—wife, son, daughter-in-law, and grandchildren—and a younger man he introduced as his relative.

Nasar asked, "So who's this with you, Menon Sir?"

"He's my nephew, here on a visit visa," answered Menon Sir. The young man greeted them all with a polite smile.

"Is he looking for a job or just visiting?" Aravindan wondered.

"I'm here to look for work," the newcomer said, adding with a tinge of pride, "I'm a graduate."

Ikka, cooking in the kitchen, overheard and answered sarcastically, "You picked a great time to job-hunt in Dubai."

"Exactly," said Menon Sir with a nod. "When half the world's losing their jobs, it's tough to find one. But try telling that back home. They think we're just making excuses."

"Sir, care for a drink?" Jose asked, topping off a glass.

"No, those days are behind me," Menon Sir answered. "My wife and I have to watch our son's kids when he and his wife go off to work."

Jose, already slightly inebriated, blurted out with his usual insensitivity, "Oh, so you're the babysitter now?"

The older man looked taken aback, and Jose pressed on, "I thought only folks in Europe and America brought their parents over to babysit. Didn't know that trend had arrived in Dubai."

Normally, when Menon Sir talked about his family, it was just casual chatter. He hadn't expected the conversation to turn so personal. An awkward pause settled over the group until Aravindan broke in, "So, what brings you by, Menon Sir?"

"I came to see if you can accommodate my nephew here," he explained, gesturing to the young man at his side.

"There's no free bed at the moment," said Nasar, who managed the room, "but someone's away on vacation. Your nephew can use that spot until he's back."

"Great," Menon Sir replied. "He'll join you all tomorrow."

After Menon Sir and his nephew left, Mujibukka set dishes on the table and remarked, "Menon used to be a high-ranking official at the National Bank of Dubai. Look at him now."

"When people get old, they can end up lower than a dog," Jose slurred, clearly feeling the effect of the alcohol.

"I won't wait to grow old," said Aravindan, a driver by profession. "I'd sooner crash my vehicle and be done with it."

"If you keep drinking like this," Ikka teased, "you won't need a collision to finish you off."

They all burst into laughter, and just then, the door swung open.

"The Siamese twins have arrived," Nasar announced.

Anup and Unni, who worked for a Security Company, stepped inside. They always commuted together, having the same shift times at the same company. They also happened to be about the same age, which earned them the nickname "Siamese twins."

Their arrival usually lit up the place. They had a knack for jokes and playful jibes, and they often poked fun at Ikka. He took it all in stride, never losing his temper—even when they really pushed his buttons. After all, he had a son around their age back in Kerala.

"Welcome, guys!" Jose greeted them. "The room was dull without you two. Liven things up."

"It's almost midnight," Aravindan teased, grabbing the cake from the fridge. "Time to slice it and ring in the New Year."

But something was off with the "Siamese twins," who stood by silently. Sensing their gloom, Ikka asked, "Anup, you and Unni look down tonight. What's going on?"

Anup pulled a piece of paper from his pocket. "Check out this New Year's present," he said, handing it over. "Unni got one, too."

Aravindan scanned the paper, and his face stiffened in shock. "What's wrong?" Ikka asked. "You look like you've seen a ghost."

"They've lost their jobs," Aravindan said slowly. "That's what it says. No more work for either of them."

Stunned silence followed. "How can that be?" Ikka blurted. "No warning at all?"

"They should have given a month's notice," Nasar remarked. "It's unfair to fire you like this without warning."

"Our company's not big on following labor laws," Unni explained. "Our local sponsor is influential, and the Indian partner uses that to do whatever he wants."

"I wish they had at least given us time to look for something else," Anup said quietly.

Jose, still tipsy, blurted out, "What good would more time do? It's not like employers are lining up to hire you."

"Jose, cut it out," Ikka scolded. "They just lost their jobs. Show some sympathy."

Jose erupted in coarse laughter. "Sympathy? They're adults. If you lose your job, you move on and handle it like a man."

"You'll see how it feels if you end up unemployed," Ikka snapped.

"What did you say?" Jose growled, weaving unsteadily toward Ikka. "You think I'll lose my job? I'll kill you— age doesn't matter!"

Jose lifted his hand to strike, but Anup grabbed him from behind. In the same instant, Unni aimed a swift kick at Jose's stomach, sending him crashing to the floor with a pained shout.

From outside, they heard cheers and clapping in the neighboring apartments. People were shouting "Happy New Year!" The clock had struck midnight, and the year 2009 had begun with a bang.

CHAPTER 27

Safiya looked up, startled, when the door opened to reveal a man hardly older than her own son. He carried himself with an uncommon poise, unlike most first-timers she had seen.

She had been trapped in this grim place for months. She had witnessed enough to sense what kind of customer she was dealing with, simply by watching his approach, listening to him speak, or feeling how he laid hands on her.

Pakistanis and Africans, in her experience, often showed a harshness she could never get used to. They acted as though they'd never touched a woman, taking whatever they wanted, far beyond the time allotted. They were quick to violence, quick to perversions.

Indians, especially those from Kerala, were easier in comparison. Some who discovered she was Malayali would lower their eyes in embarrassment. Usually, Indians had an extra fear of the police—making them hurried, taking what they came for, and then disappearing just as quickly.

Arabs showed up less frequently, but when they did, they brought violent whims she had never imagined. They forced her into unspeakable acts, and if she resisted, they grew hostile. Safiya couldn't complain to Reji; he feared the Arabs as much as she did, and they likely paid a higher price for their desires.

She could easily tell when a client was new to this world. Inexperienced men revealed their nerves through clumsy talk, asking her name or where she was from in an attempt to seem at ease. She never gave them the truth, of course. But the young man before her now seemed unusually self-assured, no trace of that first-time anxiety in him at all.

Safiya wondered, just for a moment, why she even bothered thinking about such distinctions when her job boiled down to offering her naked body to any client, no questions asked. She was instructed to give them thirty minutes; after that, it was her responsibility to send them away. Any delay on her part meant punishment falling on her, not on them.

There were eight women in the apartment altogether, most having been caught up in Reji's net. Safiya rarely saw them except during those brief instances when she was allowed out for urgent reasons. To her, they looked like walking corpses.

She did learn, however, of another Malayali woman among them named Elsy from Thrissur. Elsy had been lured by Reji in Kerala under the pretense of love, culminating in a marriage. After arriving in Dubai, Elsy discovered who he really was. Like Safiya, she also suffered assault and hunger until she finally caved in.

From bits of conversation, Safiya gathered that the others had stories even darker than hers and Elsy's—except for two who had joined up voluntarily. One was a Pakistani, divorced and left with no recourse but to sell her body for survival. She lacked education, had no family, and no other choice. The other was a Syrian woman, once abused by her own father, which set her on this path.

These two also served wealthy clients outside the apartment, so there was no concern about them running away. They earned high pay, and because they catered to influential men, it explained why the Shurtah never seemed to raid the apartment.

It had already been a few moments since the young man came into Safiya's dingy space. She began to slip off her worn maxi when he surprised her, speaking in Malayalam.

"Don't take it off," he said, confirming Safiya's hunch that he was a fellow Malayali. In that instant, a wave of inexplicable sadness washed over her. Hearing the familiar language felt like stepping back into her homeland, as though someone intimately connected to her past stood there.

"Then what do you want?" she asked, her voice trembling with a strange tenderness. For the first time since arriving in this place, she felt as if she was addressing an actual man rather than a beast bent on devouring her.

"I came to see you," he replied. "I know Althaf, Reji's right-hand man. He told me about a new recruit from Kerala and I had to come."

"To see me?" she asked bitterly. "Am I some zoo animal you're curious about?"

Her scornful tone made the young man falter. "No, itha, that's not it," he stammered, calling her "sister" in a way that lodged itself in her heart. For a fleeting moment, she imagined—if she had a brother, might he speak to her just like this?

"What's your name?" she asked softly. Her voice wavered.

He hesitated, then said, "Iqbal."

Safiya let out a quiet laugh. "Is that really your name? No one who comes here gives their real name. We don't, either."

Iqbal averted his eyes in silence.

"We share the same faith," Safiya said. "You must realize that what goes on here is... Haram, particularly for someone as young as you."

"Please, don't misunderstand," Iqbal replied. "I have a reason for coming, but physical pleasure isn't it."

She gave a cynical laugh. "Then what? Just wanted to watch?"

"No matter what I say, you likely won't believe me," he answered. "I'm a Muslim, and I won't stray from the right path."

Safiya let out a weary sigh. "All right, I'll trust you on that, but if Reji finds out your actual intentions, he'll do worse than just kick you out. They're capable of killing you."

"They can't touch me," Iqbal insisted. "I've dealt with worse—drug dealers, currency forgers."

"Why risk your life this way? Don't you have parents, sisters? How will they cope if something happens to you?"

He lowered his voice, "Itha, don't worry. I know how to protect myself."

Safiya shook her head. "You should leave now. We aren't allowed to talk this long. If someone's overheard, it's going to be trouble for both of us."

Iqbal glanced at his watch. She realized their thirty minutes were already up. Soon someone would knock, and if he was still inside, they'd kill the lights and drag him out by force.

"Whatever your reason, don't come back here," Safiya told him.

Iqbal ignored her plea and said, "What's your name, Itha? I asked Althaf, but he told me to mind my own business."

That was the last straw for Safiya. "I'm not giving you my name," she snapped, "not even the fake one we use here. Got it? You need to leave now. Or shall I call Reji and let him know you're asking odd questions?"

Iqbal's voice took on a sad note. "I swear by Allah, this wasn't my intention. But after seeing you, talking with you… it's like my own sister is suffering here."

"Go!" Safiya hissed between clenched teeth. "Don't try to trick me with kind words. I despise the very sight of men. I was foolish to feel any connection or speak to you. That doesn't mean you can take advantage. Just leave."

He nodded, turned on his heel, and rushed out, defeated. Safiya collapsed onto the bed, which still stank of sweat and semen from the last customers. She buried her face in the pillow and wept, though she couldn't say why.

Moments later, the overhead light flicked on again, signaling yet another visitor's arrival. Safiya forced herself upright, tore off her maxi, and flung it aside. Naked, she steeled herself for the next brute who would enter and have his way with her.

Chapter 28

From the balcony of his hotel room, Chandran Nair looked out at the Burj Al Arab, the world's tallest hotel, rising from waters that seemed to gently cradle its base. The sea was a bright, restless blue, mirroring a sky so clear it almost looked reversed on the surface.

He stood motionless, drifting in his own thoughts. At times, he checked into this hotel simply to isolate himself from the press of everyday life. He'd vanish from the public eye, refusing calls from anyone—family included. Only Murthy knew where he was.

In earlier days, these escapes meant sleeping as much as he liked, drinking a bit, and occasionally seeking female company. But of late, with age, he had lost his appetite for that last indulgence.

This time, though, his stay had a different purpose. He needed to cut himself off—from everyone, really, but especially from those to whom he owed money. The creditors were closing in, calling at his office and showing up at his home. He had begged them repeatedly for more time, and they had grown weary of his excuses. Many were on the brink of taking legal action against him.

"Let them file their lawsuits," Chandran Nair thought. "They won't recover anything. I might land in jail, but it's not like they'll get their money either."

Morning light now flooded the shoreline. People strolled and jogged along the dedicated track, mostly guests from Jumeirah Beach Hotel, where Chandran Nair was staying, or visitors from nearby Mina A'Salam. Nearly all were foreigners, and they looked carefree as they took in the sun and the sea.

He watched them and wondered, "Don't any of them have problems like mine? They all seem so cheerful."

Some waded into the water for a swim, likely planning to spend the entire morning at the beach.

He'd told his family he was off on a two-day business trip. He suspected they'd welcome his absence. His wife could shop endlessly, his daughter could disappear into Facebook and Instagram free from scolding about her studies.

But he worried about his son. Since that incident, the boy had withdrawn further, and his college had suspended him along with the others, bringing his education to a halt. Chandran Nair mourned the dreams he once had: he'd hoped to hand over the family business to his son once he finished engineering, with only minimal oversight. Now that vision was slipping away. He blamed himself, too, for being so wrapped up in work, while his wife was busy with her own preoccupations.

The court date was looming, and though Chandran Nair had hired a top lawyer, the outlook was grim.

Alcohol was one thing, but drugs put them on perilous ground. Dubai's laws were strict, the lawyer had warned. Still, he'd promised to do what he could.

A ring at the door pulled him from his thoughts, reminding him of the breakfast he'd ordered. Although the hotel offered a complimentary buffet in the lobby restaurant, he'd chosen room service, wanting to avoid any chance of running into acquaintances.

As the waiter spread out the dishes, he said, "Sir, if you want anything special, just let me know. I can arrange it."

Chandran Nair noted the assumption that he was another tourist on a leisurely Dubai trip, free to indulge in any pursuit—licit or otherwise. In years past, he might have done just that, with staff eager to accommodate. This time, though, his mind was in no shape for such pleasures.

When he failed to respond, the waiter lingered a moment, then left. Chandran Nair understood; the man was hoping for extra cash, like everyone drawn to Dubai's allure. Everyone found their own way to chase Dirham in this city.

After he finished eating, he checked his phone, which he'd silenced the previous evening. There were numerous missed calls from creditors, but none from his family. He'd instructed them not to call, telling them he'd be too busy, and if something urgent happened, they could reach Murthy.

But he did notice three or four missed calls from Murthy, all placed late the night before. That was unusual enough to make Chandran Nair think it must be serious. He tried calling back, but there was no answer.

"Idiot," he muttered to himself, frustration building. "He's the same as always—impossible to find when you need him."

A few minutes later, Murthy called back, and Chandran Nair demanded, "Why didn't you pick up when I called?"

Murthy cut past the complaint, speaking quickly. "I got a call from your home last night."

"Can't they leave me alone?" Chandran Nair snapped. "I'm trying to get some peace."

"It was urgent," Murthy said.

"All right, then—what happened?"

Murthy hesitated, which only made Chandran Nair more impatient. "Just tell me!"

"It's about your son," Murthy began. "He did something... really bad. I think he was on drugs. He came home smashing things and even tried to attack his mother and sister. And—"

"And what?" Chandran Nair's voice shook.

"I went over there right away," Murthy continued. "He'd cut his vein with a broken piece of glass. I rushed him to the hospital. They wanted to file a report, but a doctor I know was on duty. He agreed not to involve the police, because we can't handle another case with the one already pending."

Chandran Nair couldn't absorb the rest of Murthy's words. The phone slipped in his hand, and he collapsed onto the bed, face-down, reeling from the shock.

Chapter 29

"Maybe I should contact her," Nandakumar thought.

It had been nearly four months since Sushama left him. She hadn't bothered to call even once. Whenever he tried to reach her, her phone was always off. If he rang the landline, he'd inevitably get one of her parents. He'd ask to speak with her, but they deflected. At first, they claimed she was in the bathroom or busy in the kitchen. He knew they were lying, yet pretended to believe them and hung up.

Later, her mother told him bluntly, "She won't talk to you, Nanda. She's only grown more stubborn."

"Did I do something that unforgivable?" he asked. "Married couples have these issues. Staying angry for so long seems extreme."

Her mother snapped back, "You think your behavior was minor? Coming home drunk and assaulting your wife isn't trivial."

Nandakumar bristled at her words but kept his temper in check. "I was under a lot of stress," he managed. "Losing my job, and everything else…"

His mother-in-law scoffed, "Doesn't that embarrass you to say? Plenty of people lost jobs during this recession. Not all of them get drunk and act like brutes."

It became obvious to Nandakumar that Sushama was holding fast to her anger, emboldened by her parents' unwavering support. After that, he stopped calling. They never phoned him, either, as if he no longer existed.

He refused to beg for forgiveness. He admitted he was at fault, but he felt the blame they heaped on him went too far.

Word of his troubles reached Kerala, where his brother phoned and reprimanded him, and Nandakumar guessed his mother-in-law was responsible for spreading the story. Sushama was tight-lipped about family matters, and her father wasn't one to gossip. But her mother had a tendency to air everything.

His brother said, "You didn't leave for Dubai because you couldn't find a job here. You could've taken a government post like Achhan and me. That was your decision, sure, but now you're suffering just because you lost your job. Why not come home instead?"

When his brother finished scolding him, their father took the phone. Calm as always, he spoke with the measured tone of a sage. "Your life is in your hands," he said. "You'll make it or break it. I know you're intelligent. Use your judgment well."

Nandakumar's plan was to see how long Sushama and her parents would keep their distance. He wouldn't beg.

Yet today, he found himself thinking about her more than usual after running into some of her relatives at Carrefour in City Centre. They had visited him and

Sushama twice before; once, at Sushama's urging, he had also gone to their apartment with Sushama.

With teasing smiles, they asked, "What's up with you two? We keep calling Abu Dhabi, and Sushama's always there. Already had enough of each other?"

He grinned stupidly, pretending not to catch the drift of their remarks. They left, seemingly pleased at having poked fun at him.

That was when he wondered if he should finally call her. The separation was dragging on, and he was tired of fielding awkward questions. If they truly didn't want him, he would accept it and move on.

He presumed that, since he was unemployed, Sushama's parents worried about her living in hardship. He assumed they were the ones influencing her to remain so stubborn. He couldn't think of any other explanation for her unwillingness to return.

Nandakumar felt certain he would secure another job eventually. He believed the recession was gradually lifting from the market. Those who had been involved in shady dealings had fled, and banks were no longer handing out loans without sufficient collateral, thanks to the Central Bank's measures. That single action had curbed reckless spending and the failures to repay on time.

The government had also stepped in, restarting various stalled construction projects in Dubai. Stock prices for companies were on the mend. "Dubai won't ever fall behind," Nandakumar told himself.

As soon as he returned home, he phoned Abu Dhabi without even changing his clothes. Sushama's father answered, and for the first time in a while, there was no trace of anger in his voice—perhaps because it had been so long since they'd last spoken.

They both seemed to share the same question. Sushama's father asked, "How much longer will you two live apart?"

Nandakumar responded, "Ask your daughter that."

Her father hesitated. "We've tried—do you think we enjoy her being away from you? What can we do when she threatens suicide if we press her to go back? No parents can disregard something like that."

Nandakumar felt rattled by the comment. "I see. I wrongly assumed you two were the cause of her stubbornness."

"No, we never wanted to keep her away. Yes, we were upset when we learned you'd hurt her, and that explains her mother's strong reaction when you spoke. Please don't take offense," he said.

Nandakumar considered that. Could a simple apology fix the harm he'd caused? He believed parents should give married children the space to solve their own problems, stepping in only sparingly. That would help them work things out on their own.

But he kept those thoughts to himself. Instead, he said, "I'll come see her. If she won't return willingly, I'll bring her back to Dubai by force."

Sushama's father laughed. "You should have done that sooner."

Nandakumar gave a small chuckle of his own. "I guess my wisdom took its time coming."

CHAPTER 30

For the first time in months, Safiya heard the call to prayer from a nearby mosque. She rose from her bed, performed her ablutions, and prayed Fajr. Afterward, she recited her dhikr and salat, raising her hands in supplication to Allah.

"Ya Rabbul aalameen, thank You for rescuing me and restoring peace to my wounded mind and body. I had begun to lose faith in prayer. I believed there was nothing left to hope for, that I would remain a vessel for others' desires until I died from some illness."

Tears coursed down her cheeks as she knelt there, losing track of time. These were not tears of sorrow, but of gratitude. She felt as though a vast sea of solace had carried her safely to shore.

She was certain now that God's mercy comes eventually to those who yearn for it with sincerity. Not once had she imagined she could ever escape from Reji's clutches. It felt like a dream, and she could scarcely believe it was real.

Iqbal started visiting her more frequently, ignoring all her warnings. If Safiya was busy with another customer, he'd simply wait. Reji and Althaf tried steering him else one, even raising the price in hopes he'd lose interest, but he willingly paid the extra amount without complaint.

Sometimes, Safiya wondered if he might be insane and asked him so, only to receive nothing more than a cheery laugh in return.

Reji, meanwhile, grew increasingly uneasy about these meetings. One day, after Iqbal had left, he barged into Safiya's room and said, "That guy who just left—who is he? Why does he keep coming here?"

"He comes like the others," Safiya replied.

"I know that. No one comes around just to look at you—you're not Aishwarya Rai. I'm asking what connection you two have. Did you know him before?"

"No," she said flatly.

"Then why all the talking? Why doesn't he stick to business like everyone else? Do you think I'm a fool?"

The next time Iqbal came to see her, Safiya warned him that Reji was getting suspicious. Iqbal gritted his teeth. "Let him suspect," he said. "Itha, you'll see. It won't be long."

"If you hate them so much, why do you keep paying them?" she asked. "Isn't that just helping them stay in business?"

"Me? Encourage them?" He laughed in that carefree way of his. "You'll understand soon."

Safiya recalled how, on one of his visits, he had leaned in close and whispered, "Itha, do you want to get out of this place? I can help you."

She'd hissed back, "Are you crazy? If they realize what you're planning, they'll kill you and no one will ever know."

Iqbal only flashed his usual grin. "Don't judge me by my age. You'll see what I'm capable of soon enough."

She'd laughed at that. By then, he no longer felt like a stranger; she had come to regard him almost as a brother, and over time, even as a son. Whenever he approached, she sometimes had the eerie sensation that her breasts beneath the thin maxi might start to lactate.

At first, she assumed he was just spinning tales. But then, one night, the CID raided the apartment.

Several young Arabs arrived wearing turbans rather than the usual khantoora and Agal. They pressed the doorbell relentlessly. Only a few rooms had customers at that hour. Safiya and some of the other women, having no guests, had gone to bed but were told to be ready in case someone showed up.

Hearing the buzzer, Safiya got up, thinking it was a late-arriving customer. She opened the door slightly and saw Reji, Althaf, and the Bangladeshi in the hallway, all looking stricken with fear. They had been refusing to open the door, despite the repeated ringing. Suddenly, someone outside began pounding it with a heavy object. Moments later, the door gave way, crashing to the floor, and CID officers charged inside.

Reji and the others tried to resist, and a brief struggle erupted. One of the officers kicked Reji square in the stomach. Althaf and the Bangladeshi were thrown to the ground. They scrambled back to their feet, only to be knocked down again by more blows.

Safiya watched with a quiet sense of justice as the officers subdued Reji and his lackeys. These were the same men who had beaten the women so many times, and she took some solace in seeing them taste a bit of their own cruelty.

The CID gathered everyone, including the customers, restraining them in handcuffs and shackles. Not long after, a team of female officers arrived with a van to transport the women to a government-supported shelter—Safiya's current refuge.

Once at the shelter, a female doctor examined each of the women, taking blood samples for tests like AIDS. They were given new clothes and, for the first time in months, Safiya found herself able to rest through the night without fear.

Upon rising for her morning prayers, she picked up a Quran that an Arab lady running the shelter had given her. Though she couldn't understand the lady's Arabic, a Malayali woman who cleaned at the shelter translated: Safiya should praise the Creator for every chance at deliverance. The woman also mentioned how rare it was to break free from men like Reji. In that moment, Safiya silently offered thanks to Allah.

Althaf had occasionally been kind enough to let her phone home using his mobile, urging her not to let Reji find out. Speaking to her children had filled her with hope even as her tears spilled over; At that time, she thought she might never see them again. But now, she was free from that brutal grip.

Clutching the Quran against her chest, Safiya's heart brimmed with gratitude for her newfound liberty.

Her prayers had not gone unanswered. That evening, while watching television in the recreation room, the security guard informed her that someone was waiting in the visitors' area. She arrived to find Iqbal, wearing the same easy smile he'd always worn when visiting her in the apartment.

"Do you believe me now?" he asked—the young man who had freed all those trapped women. To Safiya, he was more than a savior; he felt like a brother, even a son, sent by Allah to rescue the forsaken.

Fighting back tears, she warned him to watch out for Reji and the others—they could still seek revenge.

"They're behind bars," Iqbal said gently. "Human trafficking charges can keep them locked up for over a decade. All their associates have been taken in, too."

She shook her head in amazement. "How did you make that happen? I assumed your talk was just talk."

He explained that a Yemeni coworker—referred to as a Mandoob in his company—was devout. Iqbal had confided in him, and the Mandoob alerted the authorities.

"What you did is incredible," she murmured. "May Allah reward you. My children and I will always pray for you."

"Itha, then you'll just have to pray harder," Iqbal teased, handing her an envelope.

"In case you're wondering," Iqbal began, "that envelope holds a plane ticket back home, as well as a demand draft you can cash at your bank there."

At those words, Safiya felt a surge of relief wash over her, a feeling that only deepened when she realized she could finally leave behind the nightmare she'd lived. She had almost forgotten she was a person. Her mind and body had been coated in shame.

Yet she had to keep going for her children. They'd lost their father and had only her to depend on, so she'd do whatever was necessary to care for them and give them a decent life.

Iqbal explained further, "We're making arrangements so you can leave quickly, without getting entangled in legal formalities. You'll hear soon. Then, all you need to do is present this ticket at the counter, and you'll be on your way."

He pointed toward a suitcase in the corner of the visitors' area. "Itha, you can take this when you travel. It's full of clothes and necessities for you and your children. Keep it in your room for now."

Safiya's eyes brimmed with tears. "You must have spent so much on all of this," she said.

Iqbal shook his head gently. "I'm not doing this alone. It's part of an organization I work with, dedicated to helping people like you. Remember, I told you I had plans for you? This is what we do."

She couldn't hold back her emotions any longer. She pulled him into a tight embrace, weeping uncontrollably. This time, he didn't answer with his usual laugh. He simply wept with her.

Chapter 31

He received a letter from home that afternoon, delivered by the roommate who had just returned from vacation. It was a reply to a letter he himself had sent, choosing old-fashioned correspondence instead of a phone call for the first time in a long while. Though the envelope arrived in the morning, he lacked the courage to open it until evening, certain its contents would upset him. At last, he decided to face it and read.

His heart churned like restless waves at the words he found, as disheartening as he had feared. Luckily, no one else was in the room just then. Otherwise, they would have seen his disappointment and pelted him with questions.

Their shared space housed a variety of personalities. Some were kind, others foul-tempered. A few had decent salaries, while the rest struggled on meager wages. Despite this, they coexisted in relative harmony. Should anyone seem despondent, the others rallied around, offering comfort. If someone fell ill, they prepared gruel and shared medicine. Yet they were also prone to heated arguments over trivial matters, snapping at each other without warning.

Now, seated on the carpet, Mujibukka leaned back against the wall and stretched his legs in front of him. His hands moved over them, trying to soothe the constant ache—especially in his knees—that had plagued him for months. Sloan's Balm and Tiger Balm hadn't helped, and he hadn't gone to a doctor. He didn't have the money for doctor's fees or prescriptions, and a government hospital wasn't an option without a valid health card.

He was over sixty and had spent three decades in this desert land. For all those years, every decision he made was about providing for his wife and children, never about his own comfort. He had taken on any odd jobs he could get, since he wasn't educated and had to make do with whatever was available. Nearly every Dirham he earned was sent home, with only a small amount kept back for his own survival.

Gradually, he had replaced their old hut with a proper concrete house and arranged respectable marriages for his three daughters. He had even helped his son launch a small business of his own. At some point, he realized that all his personal comforts had been sacrificed for his family.

He often thought of retiring, believing he deserved some rest after so many years of hard work. Yet when his wife insisted on visiting Dubai just for fun, he knew his rest would have to wait. He couldn't talk her out of it, no matter how much he explained the expense.

To bring her here, he arranged a three-month visit visa and a plane ticket, then covered her living costs and shopping bills—including the gold she wanted. He borrowed heavily to manage it all.

Then his daughters also decided they wanted to see Dubai. He paid for each of their trips separately, along with the costs for his grandchildren. He considered himself lucky that none of his sons-in-laws had shown interest in coming, or his debts would have soared even higher.

His earnings fell short of covering these mounting costs. Although he had tried various jobs, he ended up working as a cook. He prepared meals for three different bachelor quarters, getting five hundred Dirhams from each, and in addition he cooked at the quarters where he lived in exchange for food and shelter.

But age was catching up with him. Every evening, pain throbbed through his limbs. Cooking for ten to fifteen people in three separate places was no easy task, especially when hardly anyone bothered to help in the kitchen. Despite his years, he had no choice but to handle everything on his own.

All of these hardships had prompted him to write a letter home – something he hadn't done in ages. Usually, he made do with cheap internet calls instead of putting pen to paper. But this time, he wanted to be sure his predicament came across clearly, and a phone call didn't seem sufficient.

In his letter, he laid out his struggles, his weariness, and his wish to return home for good. The response now in his hands had been written by his son on behalf of the family. While acknowledging his father's wish, the son requested him to find a high-paying Gulf job for himself, so he could "manage family matters" once his father retired.

"Ass," he muttered through clenched teeth. "A proper fool." This son had already wasted large sums in the name of running a business, always complaining about losses and begging for more money to restock.

Mujibukka had a special fondness for his son, the only boy after three daughters. Even though he hesitated each time he sent his son money, his heart would soften, and he'd scrape together what was asked, often borrowing to do so. He knew his son wasn't managing any real business and was merely squandering money on unimportant things.

"He wants to come to Dubai?" he grumbled under his breath. "As though people here are just waiting to hand out lucrative jobs! A 'well-paying job' is what he expects, but the boy never studied well, and he's not one for hard work. While the neighborhood kids attended school and college, he ran around with that Mammootty Fans Association nonsense."

The door opened, and Anup stepped in. He looked a shadow of his former self after a month of fruitless job-hunting. Ever since he was suddenly let go from the security company, he'd been scouring the city for work, desperate to land something before his company-mandated grace period ended.

Unni, his close friend, had gone back home after collecting what little end-of-service pay the company provided, thus splitting the "Siamese twins"—one still in Dubai, the other back in Kerala.

"How's the job search going, son?" Mujibukka asked gently.

Anup shot him a weary glance. "Ikka, do you have to ask me that every single day? I'm sick of giving everyone the same discouraging answer."

Mujibukka tried to soothe him. "I ask because I'm hoping one of these days, you'll say you've found something. I want so badly to hear that."

Mujibukka pondered the state of things in Dubai. Countless people had lost their jobs, and many, like Unni, had gone home. But not everyone could leave. Some had pending credit card bills or personal loans. If they tried to slip away without paying, they'd be nabbed at the airport and end up in jail rather than back in their villages. Others owed money in their homeland, often for visa or travel expenses, and would face their own share of trouble upon returning.

Having changed out of his sweaty clothes, Anup dropped down on the carpet beside Mujibukka. He smelled strongly after wandering the city the entire day, but that didn't bother Ikka.

"Did you get a chance to eat anything?" asked Mujibukka.

"How could I?" Anup replied wearily. "At least in Kerala, you find public taps for water. Here, I'd have to buy it, and I'm broke."

His words tugged at Mujibukka's heart. "Then why not go back like Unni, take whatever end-of-service settlement they offer? Even if you have to do some manual labor at home, that might be better than struggling here. You're still young—you can start over."

Anup almost burst into tears. "I've thought about it a hundred times, Ikka. I really could have gone home. But if they see I've lost my job, nobody'll open mu house door for me—not even my own mother."

"You're right," said Mujibukka. "They want our money, not us."

He pushed himself up from the floor with care. "Wait here. I'll fix you something to eat."

Anup let out a weary sigh. "But Nasarkka and Jose told me there's no more food for me unless I pay what I owe."

"When did they say that?" asked Mujibukka, sounding surprised. "Don't worry about it. You can share mine. One person can't eat for two, but two can usually stretch a meal meant for one."

Anup felt a lump in his throat. "Ikka, who are you, really? My father from some past life?"

"Why not claim me in this life, too?" Mujibukka teased. "I'll just think of myself as having two sons."

Chapter 32

Abdu's sister's wedding day inched closer, and he felt lost about what to do. He had been the one to push for the date, despite his father's suggestion to wait until Abdu could return home on leave. Abdu had been certain that Chandran Sir would grant him time off and help with the costs, because Chandran Nair often mentioned how Abdu's father stood by him in his darkest days, at a time when no one else would.

Although there was no dowry involved, the bride needed twenty-five sovereigns of gold, a monumental expense given the rising gold prices. The groom, too, had his own sister to marry off and insisted on waiting until her wedding was settled. Some proposed doing both weddings at once, but he felt it wouldn't be right to stand as a groom while also handling his sister's wedding arrangements.

This search for a match for his sister dragged on, delaying Abdu's sister's wedding date. Abdu, though, welcomed the delay—it gave him more time to raise the hefty sum required. He had been living frugally for months, pinching every Dirham and skipping even minor indulgences, like a can of Pepsi, no matter how parched he got.

After the groom's sister's wedding ended, pressure mounted on Abdu's family to finalize a date for his sister's marriage. So Abdu told them to pick any date that suited them, confident he would secure leave and make it home in time. Eventually, a day was set – now only a week away.

Yet things were falling apart at the company. Chandran Nair moved around like a man on the verge of a breakdown, and Abdu heard rumors that the business was nearing collapse. At first, he dismissed such talk as idle gossip, but the signs were too strong to ignore. A wave of layoffs had hit, creditors were turning up at the office daily, and Abdu even caught wind of potential legal trouble for Chandran Nair, though he couldn't confirm it. Still, it seemed entirely possible.

In such chaos, Abdu began to doubt the security of his own job. He didn't dare ask for leave now; and even if they granted it, he was uncertain the company could afford his flight ticket. He'd been overdue for vacation for two years, which should entitle him to a ticket and leave salary—plus his unpaid wages for the current month. This money was crucial for his sister's wedding. He had also hoped Chandran Nair might give him a small bonus, which would save him from borrowing altogether. But as events spiraled, he felt all those plans crumbling away.

Later, Abdu vacuumed the entire office and mopped the floors, tidying the toilets and the pantry. He noticed the place was empty. Even Murthy, who used to stay late, had started leaving early these days.

Once he finished his tasks for the day, Abdu could have headed back to the labor camp after switching off the lights and locking the office, but he'd been in a gloomy mood since morning, his mind full of troubling thoughts. That slowed him down enough to miss the company van.

Now he'd have to catch a public bus to Al Quoz, delaying his return even further.

After locking the main door, he stepped into the corridor and pressed the elevator button, waiting for it to arrive. To his surprise, when the doors slid open, Chandran Nair was inside. Abdu turned to accompany him back to the office, but Chandran Nair said, "Abdu, you go on. I'll open the office myself."

"No problem, Sir," Abdu offered, "I can open it."

A moment later, Abdu found himself inside with him. He switched on the lights, then headed to the pantry. He filled the kettle, made tea, and brought it into Chandran Nair's office.

Chandran Nair was rifling through a drawer, tossing papers onto the desk. Abdu stood there holding the cup, reluctant to place it down; the frantic search might send it flying. He realized Chandran Nair was looking for something crucial and decided he'd set the tea cup on the table once the chaos had eased.

He sifted through each paper without finding what he wanted, shoved them back into the drawer, then took the tea cup from Abdu. As he drank tea, he asked, "So, Abdu, anything new?" It was a question Abdu had been bracing himself for.

He hesitated, deciding if this was the moment to mention his sister's wedding. Chandran Nair rarely came by the office these days, and when he did, he always appeared too unsettled to talk. Summoning courage, Abdu finally spoke. "My sister's wedding is in a week."

Chandran Nair looked at him, taken aback. "Oh right, I completely forgot. Your father called me last week to invite me, but it slipped my mind in all the office chaos."

Abdu tried to find the right words, but Chandran Nair beat him to it. "So, you need leave to go home and prepare, right?"

"Yes," Abdu admitted, "but I wasn't sure if it was okay to ask, given everything going on here."

"Don't worry. You can book your ticket tomorrow," Chandran Nair said. "Just tell Murthy; he'll write up the LPO for the travel agent."

He paused and then added, "Although, we do owe the travel agent some money. They might hesitate to issue another ticket."

He opened a drawer and pulled out a cheque book, then paused and put it back, as if recalling something. Abdu guessed the company account was likely low on funds and felt a wave of sympathy for his boss. He considered telling Chandran Nair not to worry about any contribution.

Abdu already felt grateful for everything Chandran had done. He vividly remembered the time his father needed surgery, and he hadn't been able to send the money. Chandran Nair had noticed his distress. "What's wrong?" he had asked. "You look upset."

Abdu tried to brush it off with a "Nothing, Sir," but Chandran Nair wasn't convinced. "I know you better than that. You don't have to hide it from me. The son of Assainarikka is hardly a stranger."

When Abdu finally revealed his father's situation, Chandran Nair had felt disappointed that he hadn't spoken up sooner. Straight away, he wrote a sizeable cheque and handed it over. Those had been the prosperous days for the company, but now the situation was far more precarious.

All at once, Chandran Nair did something Abdu never expected. He took off the hefty gold chain around his neck and passed it to him. "Sell this at Sona Bazaar," he said. "It'll cover your plane ticket and other costs. Before you leave, I'll try to put some more money together."

"No, Sir," Abdu objected. "That chain's important to you. There's no need—"

Chandran Nair gave him a gentle smile. "It's fine. Given my history with your father, I owe you much more than this. If only the times were better…"

Chapter 33

Khalifa Rashid sat quietly in the Majlis, a small chamber off the villa's veranda, wishing someone would come by to sit and talk with him. The silence dragged, and his loneliness settled in like a heavy blanket. In the past, a few old friends had visited now and then, but none showed up anymore—some had passed away, others were bedridden. He thanked God that he was still alive.

People said he was eighty, though he suspected he might be older, having never really kept track. He had spent his early years in a religious school, learning to recite the Quran, but formal schooling had been almost nonexistent. He never learned to read or write.

He shifted on the Persian rug, trying to ease the ache in his backside from sitting so long. Age had made his body frail, and he placed a pillow under his legs to get more comfortable.

He felt hungry. The servant had brought him khubz and fish saloona for lunch, but now it was nearly time for Maghrib prayer. He called out for the servant; no one answered. Khalifa suspected he'd slipped away somewhere, ignoring the old man's calls. Lately, Khalifa sensed that the servant did as he pleased, knowing no one would bother to hold him accountable.

Despite having seven children, Khalifa felt the weight of solitude pressing down on him. In his younger days, he had spent endless hours out fishing or diving for pearls, leaving almost no time for his wife or children. They all lived in poverty, and his wife couldn't bear it any longer—she eventually ran off with an Iranian. Khalifa learned about her departure from someone on a launch and had merely shrugged, thinking, "Let her go to hell."

Under pressure from relatives, he married again, only to divorce his second wife upon realizing she ignored his children. From then on, he lived by himself, raising them as best he could. Now, he regretted how little they seemed to care about him in return.

He accepted that once children were grown, they moved on with their own lives. There was no sense lamenting the path they chose. Birdlings, after all, left the nest when they were strong enough to fly. Still, he found himself alone in the modest villa that once bustled with family.

He often wondered what his fate might have been if the compassionate ruler hadn't granted him both the villa and a monthly pension. Without that help, he would likely be sleeping in the entrance of a mosque, asking strangers for food. So he prayed for the Sheikh's continued good health, grateful for the kindness that spared him such an end.

A hookah stood nearby, but its coals had gone cold. Khalifa felt like reviving it; in his younger days, he would gather outside shops with friends after work, lingering with sheesha and friendly chatter late into the night, sipping qahwa and, later, a round of Sulaimani tea. He had always loved a strong Sulaimani—brewed until the flavor turned bold.

He recalled the times when neighborhood weddings were lively affairs, complete with drums and lively dancing. He used to join in, waving a staff or even a sword, and sometimes young women performed their own traditional dances, their long hair swaying to the music. That sight had once filled him with renewed vigor. Now those memories tasted bitter, as no one bothered to invite him anymore. He stayed in the villa, feeling like an outdated relic, wondering how much longer life would drag on in this lonely way.

His children dropped by from time to time, but they never brought their spouses, and rarely the grandchildren. Khalifa wished they understood how grandparents often longed for those younger faces even more than for their own children. Whenever he mentioned wanting to see his grandkids, they offered excuses about schoolwork and modern education's demands.

He realized he wasn't alone in this predicament. Many older Emiratis, who once lived in humble huts and ate fish and dates, now felt left out in a society that had grown wealthy and changed its ways. People like him no longer seemed to have a place in this new order.

A noise at the entrance made him turn. The Malabari servant came in, and Khalifa's temper flared. "Harami, wein enta? Where have you been?"

The servant merely smiled, which only riled Khalifa further. He believed the servant was mocking him these days, and since he worked for Rashid, Khalifa's son, he followed Rashid's instructions rather than the old man's.

Khalifa had once thought Rashid was the best among his children. He was educated, business-savvy, and highly regarded by others for his shrewdness. But something, Khalifa believed, must have gone terribly wrong to land him in this predicament.

He learned of Rashid's troubles late, given his limited social ties. An old acquaintance, who used to make fishing nets in Khalifa's seafaring days, passed the news along after Friday prayers, telling him that his son was in jail for killing a woman. Khalifa initially dismissed it as a misunderstanding. He trusted his son too much to think he would ever commit murder.

Still, he had sensed unease the last time Rashid visited. Khalifa asked if anything was wrong, but Rashid only mentioned financial issues with his business. Never did Khalifa imagine a woman might be involved. He couldn't fathom why Rashid would look for another relationship when he already had a solid marriage and children. If one wife wasn't enough, Islamic law permitted a second, provided he cared for both fairly. Many Emiratis did precisely that: one local wife, another from somewhere else, such as Egypt or Morocco. Khalifa recalled that, in his youth, Arabs would even marry Malabari women from places like Calicut.

The servant interrupted his thoughts, asking if he should bring dinner, but Khalifa said he would eat after Maghrib prayer. Lately, he performed most of his prayers at home, going to the mosque only on Fridays. Even that short walk had become difficult for his aging frame.

Khalifa's spirits lifted at the sound of movement near the gate. He felt sure someone was coming in and hoped they might stop by for conversation.

He had once asked his children for a car—even a used one—and a driver so he could get around more easily. With a car, he could attend all five prayers at the mosque and roam Hamriya or Murshid Bazar in the evenings, meeting others his age, enjoying sheesha and qahwa. But his children dismissed it as a needless expense, citing the cost of buying and maintaining a vehicle.

Khalifa squinted into the growing dimness in the portico, certain he'd seen someone cross the yard. Where had they gone? Fear prickled along his spine. Could it be Azrail, the Angel of Death, come to collect his soul in this lonely moment, without a single loved one nearby? Convinced his life was nearly at an end, he murmured the Kalima Shahadah—"La ilaha illallah! Muhammad rasoolullah!"—and at that moment, the call to Maghrib prayer drifted from the mosque.

"Ya Rabb," Khalifa whispered in a trembling voice, "make my grave a place of peace... and grant me a place in Your Jannatul Firdaus..."

Chapter 34

Doctor Ali sat silently for a long moment, eyes on the lab report, while the faint hum of the air conditioner pressed against the stillness. Nandakumar felt his unease mount, sensing something amiss in these results from his recent blood and urine tests. He wondered why the doctor remained so quiet.

Eventually, the doctor broke the silence. "Looks like you've been drinking a bit too heavily," he said at last.

"Is there a problem?" Nandakumar asked, feeling a knot tighten in his stomach.

Doctor Ali lifted the report and tapped it lightly. "That's what it suggests. Traces of liver damage. You've been overdoing it."

Nandakumar tried to explain. "Doctor... you know how it's been since I lost my job. I just—lost control."

The doctor gave a wry laugh. "A lot of folks in Dubai are out of work these days, Nanda. They don't all pick up a bottle and wreck their health. The recession's hit everyone. Remember this clinic a year ago? You needed a token and still had to wait hours. Now, it's nearly empty."

"True, I noticed the difference," Nandakumar said quietly. "The waiting area was almost empty; I walked straight in."

"That's exactly it," said Doctor Ali. "The recession has driven people away. Many lost their jobs, canceled their visas, and left the country. So, patient numbers dropped. But you don't see me drowning my worries in a bottle."

Nandakumar's voice lowered. "I've been dealing with some family issues…"

The doctor let out a dry laugh, as if Nandakumar had just told a joke. "Money strains, wounded pride—of course that puts pressure on family life."

"That's not what I meant," Nandakumar clarified. "My drinking caused trouble with my wife."

"Ah," Doctor Ali replied knowingly. "Then you understand: it's not just your health that suffers. It hurts your home life, too. You have to give it up."

Nandakumar took the prescription and left the clinic, determined to never touch alcohol again. Driving home, he recalled instances when Sushama seemed uncaring because of his unemployment. He believed she left him, fearing life wouldn't be as easy anymore, now that he was out of a job.

But almost as soon as he let those thoughts form, Nandakumar regretted them. He felt angry at himself for judging her so harshly. He knew that, for all her beauty, Sushama was innocent and trusting, quick to believe whatever she was told. And if someone said something that conflicted with what she'd heard before, she'd believe that, too. She just wasn't worldly enough yet, he thought.

He had already decided to visit Abu Dhabi, having spoken with her father, who seemed ready to welcome them back together. Her father had been calling often, wondering why Nandakumar was taking so long to come for her. The parents' anger seemed to have cooled with the time she'd spent away, and Nandakumar suspected they worried he might eventually decide on a divorce if things went on like this. No parent wanted that for their daughter.

Still, he didn't plan to bring her home just yet. He'd been interviewing with several companies, and some made him promising offers. These were reputable firms, and with a little negotiation, he hoped for a higher salary. His plan was to show Sushama the appointment letter once his terms were settled, so she'd see a clear future.

He pictured that day eagerly. He wanted her parents to understand he wasn't worthless—losing one job didn't mean he couldn't find another, and there'd be no forced homecoming as they might have feared.

Recalling Dr. Ali's counsel, Nandakumar resolved to take back control of his life. Even Dubai's economy, he thought, was beginning to recover from the recession—so why couldn't he do the same? He truly meant it when he promised never to drink again, and he planned to watch his diet, not wanting to become chronically ill at this relatively young age.

That night, lying in bed, he found his thoughts drifting back to his mother for the first time in many years. She had passed away when he was only eight, yet until then, she had showered him with constant attention and care.

She'd longed for a daughter after having her first child, a son, and she'd been disappointed to have Nandakumar—

another boy. Making up for it, she sometimes dressed him in girls' clothes, which made him chuckle at the memory now.

He rose from the bed and pulled out an old photo album, one that Sushama had filled with their childhood pictures. Among them were snapshots of little Nandakumar decked out in frocks and skirt-and-blouse sets.

He remembered how he and Sushama would laugh, flipping through those photos. She'd point at him in his girlish outfits and tease, "How humiliating!" and he'd shoot back, "Check out your own photo—no underwear in sight! What a scandal!" She'd try to snatch the picture to tear it up, and he would stop her, saying, "Leave it. They're fond memories."

Nandakumar slipped the album back into the wardrobe. Instead of returning to bed, he slid the balcony door open and stepped outside, resting his arms on the railing. A dark sadness stirred within him. He remembered how proud he'd once been—his prestigious job, his handsome salary. But now he realized that reputation and wealth were fleeting comforts. Without peace of mind, everything else felt hollow.

A gentle breeze grazed his face, and he wondered what Sushama might be doing in Abu Dhabi at that moment. Was she lying awake, as restless as he was, or did she sleep soundly and dreamlessly? He couldn't fathom how she had managed so long apart.

He went back inside and dialed his home in Kerala, forgetting that it was already after midnight in Dubai, an hour and a half ahead. Despite the late hour, his father picked up promptly, sounding worried. "Son, is everything all right? Why call so late?"

Hearing his father's voice, Nandakumar felt a surge of emotion that nearly choked his words. When he finally spoke, his voice wavered. "It's nothing, Achha," he said. "Nothing at all…"

He sensed that his father could hear the sadness in his voice, because he asked, "Is something on your mind, son? Is there a problem?"

Nandakumar answered honestly, "I was thinking about Amma… and I just wanted to talk to you."

"That's perfectly all right," his father reassured. "I've been meaning to call you for a few days. I know you must feel lonely without Sushama around. You should go to her and bring her back. She's a gentle soul."

"Yes, Achha," Nandakumar said quietly. "I'm sorry if I woke you."

The old man gave a kind laugh. "At my age, a sound sleep is a rare thing. Listen to me: say a prayer and rest. Don't let your sadness grow; your mother's spirit will sense it."

After hanging up, Nandakumar sank onto the bed, burying his face in the covers and weeping like a child.

Chapter 35

After seeing off his wife and daughter at the airport, Chandran Nair drove to his office instead of home. The clock had already ticked past midnight, and the security guard in the lobby stared at him in surprise. He paid no attention, heading straight for the lift. It was his first time coming to the office at such an hour, and the guard's curiosity was clear.

The elevator arrived quickly. Stepping inside the dimly lit office, Chandran felt a sudden, uneasy flutter in his chest, like he was trespassing in a place that no longer welcomed him. It was as though phantom figures lurked around every corner, mocking him in hushed tones.

In his mind, they whispered, "You're finished, Chandran Nair. All you built was a house of cards, and now it's scattered in the wind. Here you stand in the wreckage."

He flicked on the lights, one row at a time, and wandered the office. It felt like a cemetery to him—workstations like crosses marking forgotten graves. He understood then that the dreams he once held lay buried in these walls.

He also knew he would never return. "It ends tonight," he thought. Once more, he walked the length of the office before going into his cabin.

For the past week, he hadn't been to the office, nor had he engaged in any of its daily affairs. He'd ignored Murthy's repeated calls. Instead, he had spent his days in and around the Dubai Justice Court, weighed down by his son's legal troubles. Though he had hired one of Dubai's best attorneys, all he heard was "We'll do our best." He had spent what little money he had left on legal fees and related costs, and now there was nothing.

It had all come to nothing. Lab reports confirmed, beyond doubt, that the students had not only been drinking but taking drugs too. The court handed down a ten-year sentence to his son and the others. Hearing the verdict, Chandran Nair felt the ground vanish beneath him; he slumped onto a nearby bench, unable to stand.

He didn't even get to see his son before they led him away. Chandran Nair had already resolved that once his son was released, he would send him, along with his wife and daughter, back to Kerala. Now, he'd be sending the two of them off without him.

His wife resisted leaving without their son, but Chandran Nair convinced her that their boy was only detained for questioning and would be out soon. Both his wife and daughter believed the story he spun, and that belief made it easier for him to proceed.

Life in Dubai had taken a toll on them. Creditors were showing up at their home, demanding money. His son's issues piled higher each day; he returned home drunk, ignored every warning, and locked himself in his room, refusing to face his father. The credit card was overdue, which meant his wife could no longer shop as before. Household expenses had grown unmanageable, and his daughter's school fees remained unpaid. Even the grocery bills and the maid's wages were left hanging.

Chandran Nair feared he would soon follow his son to jail. Court hearings seemed lined up one after another, and he found no relief in the thought that both father and son might be behind bars at the same time. The shame of it weighed heavily on him.

He thought back to the years when he had fought against every hurdle and come out on top. Those days felt like a distant memory now. He lacked the will or the energy to take on another battle. Age had caught up with him, and a grim reality was closing in.

He owed millions in dirhams, and just as much was owed to him, but those indebted to him were nowhere to be found. He had never pursued them through legal channels. Meanwhile, his creditors showed no mercy at all—no flexibility or patience.

He had hit absolute rock bottom. His bank account was drained, and in addition to that, he was in debt to the bank itself. He had outstanding credit card balances and unpaid rent for both his villa and his office. The weight of these obligations left him with nowhere to turn.

The BMW he used to drive was already sold. At least he had managed to settle most of his employees, ensuring they returned home without incident and that each received what was legally due to them. He had also given Abdu some extra money for his sister's wedding.

Now Chandran Nair sat on the opposite side of his usual desk, opening a notepad. Sweat beaded on his brow, despite the air conditioner blasting at its lowest temperature. Anxiety coursed through him, heating his body from within. He felt thirsty but couldn't summon the energy to walk to the pantry and fetch water.

He wasn't certain how to begin the letter. He had intended to fight as long as he could, determined to find a path out of his troubles, and only wave the white flag when every option was gone. Now that moment had arrived. He was ready to lay down his arms and give in to whatever fate held.

Should I write in English? The question crossed his mind. Though he understood some English and could speak it passably, writing was a different story. He wasn't well-schooled—his childhood had been fraught with hardship—and he doubted he could manage a proper letter in English.

In the end, he decided to write in Malayalam. He realized that whoever discovered the letter would likely have it translated for the police. Perhaps Sathyamurthy would be the one assigned to do so. A pang of regret hit him when he thought of Murthy, who had served him faithfully for so many years. He had done little in return for the man, and it pained him. It often seemed to Chandran Nair that in this land, those who truly deserve better recognition go overlooked, while the unworthy prosper. He hoped Murthy would forgive him.

He almost picked up the phone, longing to hear Murthy's voice one last time. Sincere, dependable people like Murthy were a rarity in Dubai. Time and again, Murthy had quietly done him favors, never stooping to malice or self-interest, always warning him when he was veering off course. Chandran Nair knew that ignoring those warnings had cost him dearly.

Suddenly, he remembered the old diary he kept in the drawer—his personal account book for many years. He felt the urge to see it one final time. Ever since coming to Dubai, he had meticulously written down every minor expense, every transaction.

Pulling the frayed notebook from the drawer, he felt a sharp twinge in his chest. "Oh God," he murmured. "I've recorded every single detail, yet my calculations have all failed me in the end."

Chandran Nair flipped to the first page of the diary, the one that captured his very first contract: "Ten thousand dirhams, expenses: four thousand nine hundred, profit: five thousand one hundred…"

The next page detailed the following contract, a larger deal than the first. Turning further, he saw entries of still-higher amounts. But as he kept going, the numbers declined again. On the final page, the balance read zero…. Zero.

He shut the diary and dropped it into the waste bin by his desk, convinced that his life was likewise about to spiral down to nothing.

He braced himself to write. Whispering God's name, he lamented his fate: to die here, in a foreign land, far from everyone he cared about. It felt undeserved. He had always tried to help others—giving money whenever he could, funding children's educations, and supporting the elderly in retirement homes. Now he regretted having to stop and prayed for God's forgiveness.

He told himself to stop brooding. The longer he dwelled on such thoughts, the weaker his resolve would become, and he would only face more suffering. He no longer had the strength for that.

He resolved to let his son carve out his own future once he finished his ten-year sentence. He also prayed that his wife and daughter would live as they wished. There was a house in Kerala, and his wife and daughter both had accounts with enough savings, or so he believed, to sustain them for a good while.

Now he braced himself to depart for a place free from the hardships he'd come to know. With a shaking hand, he began the first line: "I am choosing this path on my own. No one else is responsible. I see no alternative. I humbly ask everyone's forgiveness…I beg for it…"

Chapter 36

Nandakumar finally made up his mind to head for Abu Dhabi. He realized there was no point delaying any further. Every time he called home, his father urged him to bring Sushama back, warning about the gossip that was surely brewing and insisting that she'd return if only Nandakumar asked. His father stressed that he needed her more than ever now.

Indeed, Nandakumar couldn't handle living alone much longer. He stayed home most of the time, completely abandoning his usual visits to "Mirchi" and giving up alcohol. Johnny, his friend and confidant, was undergoing Ayurvedic treatment in Kerala, so no help there for a while.

Loneliness wasn't his only worry—his health was declining, too. According to Dr. Ali, he needed to watch his diet in addition to quitting alcohol. But Nandakumar didn't know how to cook, so restaurant food was his only option, which only made matters worse for his stomach and could lead to other health problems down the line.

Sushama's father frequently phoned from Abu Dhabi, asking why Nandakumar hadn't yet come for her despite promising. He'd add, "Nanda, she isn't refusing to call you out of anger; she's just embarrassed."

Nandakumar nearly had a deal with one of the companies he'd interviewed for—he was waiting on an appointment letter, expected in a week's time. Although he'd planned to pick up Sushama once his new job was a sure thing, the wait was eating at him. Having her gone made him realize how vital she was to his life.

Dubai seemed to be recovering, and at a pace surpassing many expectations. Projects that had stalled were springing back to life, propelled by the Ruler's unyielding resolve. His motto was that nothing was beyond reach, and Dubai's transformation served as proof: the metro project had been finished on 09-09-09 as promised – the world's first driverless train – and Burj Khalifa now stood as the tallest building in the world. The Burj Al Arab, the world's tallest hotel, remained another monument to the Sheikh's persistence.

Nandakumar awoke early to make preparations for his trip to Abu Dhabi. Months had passed since he'd last seen Sushama, and the thought of facing her filled him with a nervous unease. He wondered how she'd respond to him. Would she pick a fight or bring up every wrongdoing on his part? He hoped that wouldn't happen. From what her father had hinted, she seemed to regret the past conflict and longed to avoid it going forward.

He knew he had no right to blame her. She might have lashed out because she'd reached her breaking point. Nandakumar resolved to apologize and promise never to act that way again. He realized his behavior was indefensible, yet he tried to justify it as a lapse caused by alcohol.

Being let go from his job so suddenly had felt like plunging from a great height. He had seen himself as the company's most capable employee, yet they'd dismissed him without warning, leaving him both shocked and financially burdened. Finding new work took time, and his debts mounted.

He admitted he had taken on more than he could manage. Pride and overconfidence had led him to believe he could do anything he wanted, but he was grateful now for the lesson that life had taught him. He planned to proceed more carefully, following the rules the same way one would when driving.

He checked the refrigerator and discovered it was empty. Nandakumar had hoped to have bread, jam, and butter for breakfast. Having skipped dinner the night before, he couldn't picture making the hour-and-a-half drive to Abu Dhabi on an empty stomach. He decided he'd stop at a cafeteria along the way.

Before heading out, he opened his laptop and checked his email. His inbox was flooded with messages from credit card companies and commercial senders, but one message stood out: it was from Johnny. The note mentioned that the Ayurvedic treatment was helping his recovery, though it was expensive. He felt buried in debt.

Johnny asked where Nandakumar had been and said he knew from his last message that Sushama was still at her parents' place in Abu Dhabi. He called Sushama innocent and urged Nandakumar not to hurt her any further.

Then Nandakumar noticed an email from a company he'd interviewed with. Rather than flat-out rejecting him, they said they couldn't match his experience and skill with the budget on hand—his way of saying they just didn't want to pay for someone with his background. He reflected on how companies now avoided hiring experienced people due to the higher salaries required; they'd rather take on juniors for less. He shrugged it off, since he already had a better offer lined up.

Grabbing his keys, Nandakumar left for Abu Dhabi. At eleven in the morning, Sheikh Zayed Road was relatively quiet, the rush hour having died down. He couldn't help but recall a time when Dubai's streets were jammed no matter the hour, alive with cars even late into the night.

He pulled into a fuel station and filled up his tank, then parked and headed into the mini shopping mart. There, he grabbed a sandwich and coffee. As he was finishing his breakfast, his phone rang, and he was startled to see the caller ID—it was his old company.

He recalled that the mandoob had called the previous week, reminding him that his visa was up for cancellation. They wanted him to come in, sign the necessary form, and collect his end-of-service benefits. The company had granted him extra time before canceling his visa, but that grace period had now expired. If they canceled the visa before he started his new job, he'd be forced to return home while awaiting the next visa. He realized he needed to ask for another extension, just a few more days to sort things out.

When he answered, he expected the mandoob's voice on the other end. To his surprise, it was the company Chairman's secretary. After asking how he was doing, she explained that the Chairman wished to see him right away, adding that he was currently available.

Nandakumar was caught off guard. In all his years with the company, he had never interacted with the Chairman; everything had gone through the GM. Still, he agreed. "I'm free now. I can be there in half an hour."

"Great. See you then," the secretary replied before ending the call.

Nandakumar made his way back to his old office, curious about the Chairman's sudden request to see him, planning to continue on to Abu Dhabi once he was done. Entering the building, he noticed many new, younger faces and only a handful of employees he recognized. It was clear the office had undergone substantial changes since he'd left. He also spotted that his old office—the one he used to call his own—remained locked.

He recognized the same office boy and went over to him. "How have you been?" Nandakumar asked. The office boy gave a shaky sigh. "Not so great, sir. Ever since you left, the days have felt bleak."

"Don't talk like that," Nandakumar replied gently. "Our fortune doesn't depend on any single person—it's in God's hands."

The Chairman's office was spacious and tastefully decorated. Nandakumar spotted the Chairman, an Emirati from a prominent Jumeirah family, poring over files. He had been educated in the United States, holding a business management degree.

The Chairman greeted him with a kind smile and motioned for him to sit. Nandakumar did so without hesitation, feeling no reason to be uneasy. He was an outsider now, after all, and no longer beholden to the rules he once followed.

Nandakumar's heart pounded in anticipation, waiting for the Chairman to speak. At last, the Chairman delivered some astonishing news: if Nandakumar hadn't committed to any other employer, he could return to the company under the same conditions as before—salary, allowances, everything. He was free to resume work immediately.

Nandakumar could scarcely believe it. "Are you serious, Sir?" he asked, his voice trembling with excitement.

The Chairman offered a smile. "Yes, you can rejoin this very moment."

Nandakumar was speechless with gratitude, convinced that his prayers had been answered. This was more than he'd dared to hope for. During his time away, he'd heard rumors about troubles in the GM's office, the same GM who used to rely on Nandakumar's work while reaping all the praise. Now it seemed the upper management had finally recognized Nandakumar's true value.

"So," the Chairman asked, "what do you say? Are you coming back?"

Nandakumar was still reeling, scarcely able to articulate. "Yes, Sir," he managed, "but I'll start tomorrow morning, if that's all right."

The Chairman stood and extended his hand. "All right, then. Good luck!"

"Thank you, Sir. Thank you so much!" Nandakumar said, voice still unsteady.

Stepping out into the blazing sunshine, he hardly felt the heat. In one spontaneous motion, he tossed his car keys into the air and caught them with a confident grin before heading to the parking lot and climbing into his car. Pointing himself toward Abu Dhabi, Nandakumar couldn't help but exclaim, "Dubai, as you rise again, so do I! Nothing is impossible here—nothing is impossible in Dubai!"

About The Author

Shahul Valapattanam was born in 1953 in Valapattanam, a small town in Kerala's Kannur district. He published his first short story at the age of thirteen and has been writing ever since. Over the years, he has authored six novels and seven short story collections, many of which draw from the everyday rhythms, struggles, and quiet beauty of life in Malabar and among Malayalis working abroad.

For the past four decades, he has lived and worked in Dubai, where the lives of migrant Malayalis have been a constant presence in his stories. His writing reflects the emotional worlds of people caught between worlds, carrying home within them while learning to survive far from it.